AF472545

Over The Edge

Kimberly Gibney

AuthorHouse™
1663 Liberty Drive
Bloomington, IN 47403
www.authorhouse.com
Phone: 1-800-839-8640

© 2011 Kimberly Gibney. All rights reserved.

No part of this book may be reproduced, stored in a retrieval system, or transmitted by any means without the written permission of the author.

First published by AuthorHouse 5/13/2011

ISBN: 978-1-4567-6128-8 (sc)
ISBN: 978-1-4567-6129-5 (e)
ISBN: 978-1-4567-6130-1 (hc)

Library of Congress Control Number: 2011907845

Printed in the United States of America

Any people depicted in stock imagery provided by Thinkstock are models, and such images are being used for illustrative purposes only.
Certain stock imagery © Thinkstock.

This book is printed on acid-free paper.

Because of the dynamic nature of the Internet, any web addresses or links contained in this book may have changed since publication and may no longer be valid. The views expressed in this work are solely those of the author and do not necessarily reflect the views of the publisher, and the publisher hereby disclaims any responsibility for them.

This book was made possible through the love and support of my dear friends and family. Therefore, I dedicate the success of this amazing journey to my best friend and loving husband Eric, my angel from heaven Jacob, my ultra supportive and amazing friend Karen, my wonderful new friend and Editor Lynn, and my driving force to finally publish this book Kristen and Kim. Thank you all for your support.

Chapter 1

It was late September of Sara Grady's senior year when her family moved to the sleepy little New England town of Simpleton. Sara's father, Bill Grady, had taken the position of police chief of the town. Simpleton was a safe and somewhat boring town from what Sara had gathered so far. Most of the people had lived here their entire lives and had no idea what life was like outside of this small town. The nearest shopping mall was over an hour away—and let's face it, shopping is every teenaged girl's favorite pastime next to talking on the phone. The main reason Bill Grady had accepted the position was the non-existent crime rate—having his family in a safe community was important to him.

Her mother and older brother were thrilled for him. Sara, on the other hand, wasn't happy about being uprooted and having to start her last year of high school over again. Sara's brother was in college so he didn't have to endure the pains of getting to know a new school, friends, and just life in a small town in general.

Sara did love the new house, though. It was huge compared to the little Cape Cod she had grown up in back in New York. Her room was on the third floor; a finished attic, practically her own private apartment. At least she felt she could escape there when everything else seemed miserable in her life.

Moving to Simpleton wasn't exactly the highlight of her year. In fact,

Sara felt that leaving her friends behind would probably kill her. Thank heaven for the internet and cell phones. Sara knew she was going to have to make an effort, though, if she wanted to fit in, and not fall into the "wrong crowd". Senior year and having to start at a new high school wasn't her idea of fun. The first day was going to be the worst, but she knew she had to get through it.

The fall semester had already begun two weeks prior to Sara's arrival in Simpleton so she was a bit behind, but that wouldn't be a problem since she had a nearly perfect GPA and was counting on earning a scholarship to college. Monday morning after the move-in weekend came before she knew it. Sara showered and hopelessly ran a hand through her long hair. She pulled on her favorite skinny jeans, boots, and navy sweater. She critically looked herself over in the mirror before grabbing her keys and shoulder bag, and headed downstairs. Her mom greeted her with a smile.

"Don't you want to eat anything before you go, Sara?"

"No, too much nervous energy."

"Well, have a great day honey, and try and make some new friends."

"Will do," Sara said sarcastically, closing the kitchen door and heading out to her car.

Sara loved her car, a fully restored 1969 Ford Mustang convertible, cherry red with bucket seats. It was her Mom's first car and her grandfather had helped to restore it the summer before he passed away. This car screamed confidence and when she sat behind the wheel that knot of insecurity she felt melted away. Sara turned the key and the engine purred as she started the car. She glanced in her rear view mirror and slowly backed out of the driveway, dreading the day that lay before her.

The drive to school was shorter than she had expected. As she arrived the students were gathering in the parking lot leisurely awaiting the first bell. Sara wasn't sure exactly where to park so she took the farthest spot from the building. She felt like everyone was staring at her as she pulled in and cut the engine. The parking lot wasn't that big, so the chance that she could make an anonymous entrance was next to impossible that day. Sara took one last glance in the tiny mirror on the sun visor and opened the car door to what she expected to be the entrance to living hell. Much to her dismay and just as she had expected, everyone was staring at her. Thinking *so much for that anonymous entrance*, she put her head down, trying not to make eye contact with anyone in particular. She headed toward the front office to meet the registrar and get her class schedule. After Mrs. Peabody, the registrar, got her settled, she headed out to begin the first day of the rest of her life.

The school seemed rather large for a small town, but Sara was hopeful that she would find her way around. Things sure were different here than at her old high school. Back there, you were subject to metal detectors and people fighting in the halls. At Simpleton High, things were much different, or at least that is what she had seen so far. Sara was making her way to her locker and first period English—and not paying much attention to where she was walking—when she collided with a strikingly beautiful blond girl, dropping the map she'd picked up at the registrar's office.

"Sorry, I wasn't looking," Sara said, stopping to pick up the map from the floor.

"No problem—you look a little lost," the girl said in a nice way, despite the fact that Sara had almost knocked her on her butt. "I'm Amy. You must be Sara, right?"

"How did you know my name?"

"Small town, plus everyone has been talking about you since you pulled into the parking lot this morning. Hot car, by the way."

"Thanks," Sara said, blushing a bit.

"Let me see that schedule...we have first period together; come on, I'll show you the way."

They walked to English together and as they got to the door Sara took a deep breath before entering the classroom. Sara handed her schedule to the teacher, who gave her a copy of the novel the class had started and pointed to an open seat toward the rear of the class. The class was reading a classic and Sara's favorite, *To Kill a Mockingbird.*

Sara quickly took her seat and tried to avoid eye contact with her new classmates.

"We have a new student joining us today; please help me welcome Sara Grady."

Everyone turned and said hello. A few people from the back of the room whistled until the teacher quieted everyone down. Sara must have turned three shades of red. After her face returned to normal and class got under way she stared out the window and daydreamed her way through the rest of the class. Would she survive here in Simpleton?

The day was full of uncomfortable attention-grabbing situations like first period. When lunchtime rolled around, Sara found Amy in the cafeteria and she motioned for her to come and sit at her table. Sara recognized a few faces from some of her earlier classes—Mike, Sam, Kristen, Amy—and a bunch of other people that for now remained nameless. Sara found out that Amy was head cheerleader and that most of the people at the table either were on the cheerleading squad or the football team and for the most part pretty popular people. Sara couldn't believe she had hit the jackpot in the meeting-new-friends department on her first day. Much to Sara's surprise, everyone was very nice and really excited about the upcoming football game on Saturday against the rival high school, Chadbourn. Saturday's game was the biggest game of the school year aside from homecoming. Football in Simpleton was a tradition, and so were the victory parties. Some of the guys at the table were talking about an after party. "Dudes, we are going to Mike's lake house to celebrate afterward," Sam said to a bunch of guys that looked as though they all played on the team.

"Sara, you should come to the game," Amy said.

"I don't know…football isn't my thing."

"Come on, it will be fun and we can go to the Mike's party together afterward."

"We will see," Sara said, just to appease her.

Amy was filling Sara in on the popular crowd. As they were chatting, Sara looked up and saw a gorgeous guy walking across the room toward the table. "Who is that?" Sara asked Amy, without looking in his direction.

"That's Ethan Campbell, he is the quarterback," Amy replied with a smile.

"Oh," Sara said, trying not to make it sound too obvious that she was totally taken off-guard by his good looks.

Sara watched as Ethan joined the end of the table. The guys were all high-fiving and acting as if they were complete now that Ethan had joined them. He glanced in Sara's direction and she felt her heart skip a beat.

"He is a senior; his parents own the pharmacy in town. He also happens to drive a hot car too," Kristin joined in the conversation. Kristin Hale was co-captain of the cheerleading squad and as nice as Amy. She had long dark brown hair, olive skin, and green eyes. She looked like a supermodel for Sports Illustrated magazine. In fact she was very smart and wanted to be a psychiatrist someday.

"Does he have a girlfriend?" Sara asked, trying not to sound desperate.

Amy and Kristin smiled. "No, he is single at the moment," Amy said. The bell rang and everyone was off to their afternoon classes. Sara couldn't help but watch Ethan. He got up to leave the cafeteria with a few other guys from the team and she could have sworn he glanced back at her but it was probably just her imagination playing tricks on her. Sara thought to herself that she was not the kind of girl who swoons over the most popular good-looking guy in school. In fact, she had never dated all that much before moving to Simpleton based on the mere fact that she was rather shy. Most of the guys she knew back at her old school she had known her whole life and never thought of as anything more than friends. But Ethan was different—she could feel it. Sara watched him walk out of the cafeteria with the other guys and off to his next class.

Speaking of next classes, the next three were not so bad. In fact she was kind of getting settled faster than she had anticipated, but Biology was her least favorite subject and to end the day with biology was Sara's idea of cruel and unusual punishment.

She took her seat at an empty lab table toward the back of the class. "*Great,* she thought, *I won't have to endure a lab partner after all today.* But her luck just kept getting better—Ethan came into the class and headed toward Sara's table.

"Hey, I think you are my lab partner," he said.

"Um, if you say so," Sara replied, thinking that was so stupid.

"We haven't met, I am Ethan," he said with a drop-dead gorgeous smile.

"Sara," she replied shyly, as Mr. Stone, the Biology teacher, handed out that day's lab and everyone got to work.

The biology lab wasn't so bad, but Sara was very uncomfortable sitting so close to Ethan. Ethan Campbell, how would one describe him? He was tall, about six feet, with perfectly tousled dark brown hair, blue eyes the color of the Caribbean sea, and, from what Sara could see, a well-built body. When Ethan smiled his face seemed to draw you in and make you forget all your thoughts. Ethan was wearing faded blue jeans and a lightweight charcoal-gray sweater with brown hiking boots. He wore a class ring on his right hand and a leather band on his left wrist. Sara thought he was totally hot and looked like a Calvin Klein model on one of the billboards in Times Square.

"So you're new, huh?" he said, trying to make conversation as they progressed through the lab almost silently.

"Yeah, um…today is my first day," she said quietly.

Other people were talking rather loudly giving the indication that the lab had been completed.

"Okay people; let's keep the volume down a few decibels," Mr. Stone said.

"Your dad is the new police chief, right?" he asked, lowering his voice a bit. Ethan played with his bracelet, Sara noticed, and she wondered if he was as nervous as she was at that moment.

"Yes, I guess you know all about me, huh?" She replied, a little sarcastically.

"Sorry, I was just trying to make conversation," Ethan said, sounding defensive.

"No, I'm sorry, it's been a long day and you have no idea what it's like to tell your story fifty million times in one day," Sara said, apologizing for being rude.

"Well, I am a good listener," he said with that half grin. Sara blushed and looked down at her lab book. She could feel him staring at her but didn't have the courage to look up.

She managed to finish the lab without saying anything too foolish and without having to make direct eye contact with Ethan. The bell rang a few minutes later and everyone gathered their things and headed out of school for the day. After dropping off her books in her locker and Sara made her way to the front office to drop off the signed schedule with the registrar and then off to the sanctuary of her car.

The parking lot was the after school hangout, apparently. Everyone was congregating by their cars, listening to music, and engaged in conversation. Sara quickly made her way through the crowds to her car and tried to avoid any unnecessary contact with anyone. As she pulled out of the parking lot she gave Ethan a glance, noticing that he was getting to his car with some friends. Kristin was right about his car being hot—he also drove a Mustang, but his was a brand-new shiny black GT. Ethan watched her as she slowly pulled out of the lot and headed down the road.

"Dude, did you catch the new girl today at lunch—Sara?" Mike asked Ethan.

"Oh yeah, she was my lab partner in biology," Ethan replied.

"Why is it that you always have all the luck when it comes to the chicks at this school?" Sam asked.

"She is majorly hot; too bad her dad is the police chief. No booty calls there." Mike said.

"Dude, is that all you ever think about?" Ethan asked.

"What else is there?" Mike said, slapping high-fives with Sam.

"Her ride is awesome; did you see her looking at you?" Sam said to Ethan.

"Whatever, man," Ethan replied, slapping him on the arm as he grabbed his gear from his car. "Come on, we don't want to be late for practice or Coach will have us running laps all afternoon," he said as he watched Sara drive away.

"No way am I running laps after yesterday's practice. I think I lost my liver or something." Mike said.

"That's from all the partying you do after we win, stupid." Sam said.

It had started to rain and practice was brutal for everyone. Coach was pushing the team even harder than usual in preparation for the upcoming game on Saturday. Amy was practicing indoors with her squad to avoid the rain. Around 5:30 when practice ended the football team came through the gym cold, wet, and tired.

"You guys look rough." Amy said to Ethan and Mike.

"Man, Coach kicked our butts today. Maybe you could give me a rub down," Mike said as he sauntered toward the locker room.

"Any time, any place," Amy flirted.

"Hey Amy…come here for a second," Ethan asked. "I saw you talking with that new girl, Sara, today in the cafeteria, right?"

"Yeah, Sara is really sweet," Amy replied. "You know, she asked about you today."

"What did she say?"

"Not much, really, she just asked who you were and if you had a girlfriend."

"And…?"

"And nothing. The bell rang before she could say anything else. I told her she should come to the game Saturday and we would go to Mike's party together afterward."

"Did she say yes?"

"She said 'We will see.'"

"Convince her to go for me, OK?"

"Why, are you interested?"

"We will see," Ethan said, grinning, as he headed toward the locker room to shower.

After school Sara drove home through the downpour—even with her windshield wipers running as fast as they could she could barely see the road in front of her. She slowly pulled into the garage and turned off the engine. The day had turned cold and damp and all Sara wanted was to go up to her room and decompress. Her first day hadn't been too bad, but she was two weeks behind and she did have some reading to catch up on in a few classes. Sara didn't feel like reading at that moment so she turned on the television, threw her books on the bed, and grabbed her laptop, hoping some of her old friends were online. Leaving her old school and friends behind was even harder than she had imagined. Sara had been friends with some of those people her entire life and she felt like she was abandoning them. She logged into Facebook, expecting to chat with her friends or at least see a few questions awaiting her answer, but to her disappointment there was nothing. Sara logged off and decided to look up Simpleton High School's website. She paged through the yearbook and found Amy and Kristin's pictures everywhere; they were into lots of extracurricular activities besides cheerleading. Several pages into the senior section, she got to the football team and stopped at Ethan's picture. *Gosh, he is gorgeous,* Sara thought. Ethan was good-looking and popular, the quarterback for the varsity football team, a straight "A" student, and, most importantly, single. He was too good to be true as far as Sara was concerned and way out of her league. However, he was a fellow Mustang lover so they did have that in common. *Anyway, back to reality,* Sara said to herself setting her laptop aside. She ran her fingers through her hair wishing she had spent more time on it that morning and decided to pull her hair into her usual go-to knot. She stripped down to her underwear and changed into her yoga clothes before doing some stretches to let out her built-up anxiety from her first day of school.

Sara's cell rang as she was attempting the lotus pose and she almost pulled a hamstring answering it. "Sara, its Amy White."

"Hey, how did you get my number?" Sara asked, crossing her legs Indian style trying to work out the cramp that had worked its way into her thigh.

"School registrar; everyone has to fill out those forms."

"Aren't those supposed to be confidential?" Sara asked.

"Yeah, but I work there for extra credit so it's no big deal." Amy said.

"Oh, what's up?" Sara asked, playing with the hem of her yoga pants and thinking that it was still kind of weird that a student would have access to private information. She decided to chalk it up to small-town nosiness and let it drop.

"I was just wondering if you wanted to hang out tomorrow night. Some of us are going for pizza after practice and thought you might like to join us."

"Um yeah, I guess that would be fine."

"See you tomorrow."

"Bye."

Sara hung up her cell and sat back against her bed. *So, I have made a friend* she thought, pleased with herself. Amy looked like the typical cheerleader—blond, perfect body, and bubbly all the time. She was also smart and confident—unlike the typical teenager—and had a good head on her shoulders, as Sara would learn.

Sara's mom called up to her room, "Sara, it's dinner time."

"Be right there."

Sara's dad had come home and was washing up for dinner when she made her way down to the kitchen. Her mom, Molly, was the typical stay-at-home mom. They both shared the curse of a peachy complexion that gave away all signs of nervousness, embarrassment, and happiness. She was a great cook, too good sometimes. Sara had to watch what she ate because her Mom was always trying to fatten her and her brother up with her latest gastronomic creation.

"So, how was your first day?" Dad asked as he sat down at the table.

"It wasn't so bad." Sara replied with surprise.

"Have you made any friends yet?" Mom asked.

"I met some nice people and they invited me out for pizza tomorrow night."

"That is great, honey."

"So I hear your school has a tremendous football team. They could go All-state this year," Dad said, taking in a mouthful of roast chicken.

"I met some of them today actually," Sara said.

"Really. Anyone in particular?" Dad asked. Sara named off a few of the guys from the table at lunch, including Ethan—without trying to sound conspicuous and lead him to think she had a crush on him.

"Ethan Campbell; his parents own the pharmacy in town. I hear he is a hell of a quarterback and will most likely make state MVP," Dad said.

"I also was befriended by the head cheerleader, Amy White," Sara said, trying to change the subject and bowing her head into her plate trying to hide the blush that had come over her face. She was a dead giveaway when she liked something because her fair skin always blushed.

"I am so glad for you. So it wasn't as awful as you thought it was going to be," Mom said.

"Hey kiddo, thinking of trying out for the cheerleading team this year?" Dad asked.

"Not quite," Sara said wishing that he hadn't brought up the subject of extracurricular activities.

"I really think you should try and apply yourself this year, even if you aren't going to be on the track team." Dad said, sounding disappointed in her.

"I think I am just going to see what happens this year. Have you heard from Brian yet?" Sara asked her parents, trying to avoid further discussion of extracurricular activities. Sara had been so involved in her old school with track and student government that she never had time for other important things like dating, and she was hoping to change that this year without slacking off too much. Unlike Brian, Sara's older brother, she was never really part of the popular crowd. Brian was very popular in high school and was a part of every club, sport team, and the hottest catch on the dating scene. Despite their being almost complete opposites, Sara and her brother were extremely close. He usually called weekly to check in and see how things were going. Now that he was away at school, he only came home around the holidays and Sara missed him terribly. He knew how hard this move was on her and how she felt about starting over at a new school.

"Not yet honey, but it's only Monday. Doesn't he usually call toward the end of the week?" Dad said.

"I guess," Sara said, finishing up her dinner. She cleared her plate and helped with the dishes as usual. "I am going to finish up my homework and catch a little television before bed, so I will see you in the morning," She said to her parents, kissing them and heading back up to her room. Sara loved having her own private bathroom, unlike the old house where the family had all shared one. She showered and put on her favorite pajamas and logged onto her computer once more, hoping someone was there to chat. Sure enough, Brian was there.

"What's up bro?"

"Hey little sis." Brian said.

"Brian, I am so glad you are here."

"How was your first day? I was thinking about you all day."

"It wasn't so bad, I did meet some nice people," Sara said without giving too much detail.

"Cool deal, meet the love of your life yet?" Brian joked.

"Not quite, but there are a few prospects."

"Really? Who are they, so I can come home and beat them up for you?" He said.

"Seriously, there is one guy but he is so far out of my league."

"Listen Sara, you are a knockout and don't let anyone tell you different. If you were here at school I would be beating the guys off you with a stick."

"Keep dreaming, dork." Sara said.

"Seriously sis, have some confidence in yourself for once. By the way, any cute friends for me to meet at Thanksgiving?"

"Typical Brian, always looking for the next best thing!"

"Just keeping my options open for the holidays"

"In that case, no, and isn't Harvard crawling with girls? Haven't you met anyone special this year?"

"Not yet, but the semester is just beginning."

"How's Biology this year?"

"You mean Advanced Anatomy and Physiology?" Brian corrected her.

"Whatever, yeah. How are your classes?"

"Grueling, but I will make it through. I think I need to find someone to practice on, though." Brian said.

"Oh you are such a dork. Well, I have to run." Sara said, about to sign off.

"Talk to you soon and there is no one dorkier than you, kiddo." Brian said, signing off.

Sara saw that one of her friends had left her a message on her Facebook page saying that this year was not going to be the same without her. She couldn't help but feel the tears well up in her eyes and a heaviness build in her chest. Sara logged off for the night and wiped her eyes before climbing into bed.

Sleep would not come for easy for Sara that night despite the comfort of her room and her new bed. Sara's Mom had gone all out decorating her new room, buying her 400 thread count sheets and the softest down comforter in history. Sara tossed and turned trying to sleep but Ethan persisted in invading her dreams. His face, his smile, and his infectious laugh seemed to burn into her thoughts each time she closed her eyes. Sara dreamt of him wrapping his arms around her and kissing her in front of the entire school.

The alarm went off at 6:00 and Sara felt as if she hadn't slept more than five minutes all night. She looked in the mirror and saw the dark circles forming under her eyes. She brushed her teeth and got a nasty surprise—her gums were bleeding. She chalked it up to not flossing enough; rinsed, grabbed some clothes in an attempt to look semi-decent, tied her hair up, and headed downstairs. Sara had decided on her favorite brown cords and a low-cut red v-neck shirt with a lace cami underneath. Mom was busy cleaning the kitchen and putting away dishes from the night before as she stepped into the room.

"Got to run," Sara said, making her way toward the back door leading into the garage.

"Sara, at least drink some juice or something. You are withering away to nothing."

"I am fine, Mom. See you this afternoon," Sara said heading out the door and off to school. *I don't know how she stays so thin*, she thought fondly of her mother. *I swear if I ate half of the things she made for me I would weigh 200 pounds and then some.*

Sara's day was a little easier than the day before. People sort of got over the newness of her and just settled into routine. She still got a few long stares here and there which made her incredibly uncomfortable. At lunch, Amy convinced Sara to go to the game on Saturday and to the party at Mike's house after that despite her half-hearted protest of having other things to do.

"I promise you will have a great time," Amy said.

"And if I don't, then what?" Sara joked with her.

"Just trust me, okay?" Amy said. Everyone seemed deep in their own conversations at the table when this pretty cute guy came over. He was tall, maybe five-ten with shaggy light brown hair and green eyes. He was built well but not overly muscular. He had a deep voice which made him sound older than the average high-school guy. "You are Sara, right?" he asked Sara.

"Yeah," she said, looking up and trying to be nice.

"I'm John Waters," he said, sitting across the table from her. "So how do you like Simpleton?" Amy and Kristin gave him the evil eye but John ignored them and acted as if Sara was the only person at the table.

"Well, the verdict is still out on that one," Sara said.

"You going to the game on Saturday?"

"Um, yeah I am going I guess."

"Well, maybe I will see you there. See you later," John said as he got up and walked away. *Wow, that was a strange conversation*, Sara thought to herself.

Just then, Ethan came into the cafeteria and saw John leaving the table. He stormed over to Mike and said, "What's John's deal?"

"I don't know. Suddenly he wants to befriend the new girl," Mike said with a tone of hostility.

The bell rang and before Sara could look in his direction, Ethan was headed out the door.

Last period finally came, biology, and for once she was actually looking forward to it because she hadn't gotten to talk to Ethan at lunch today. Ethan came in as the bell rang and sat down quickly next to her. He didn't pay much attention to her and she was a little surprised after the warm welcome he had given her the day before. Maybe she was imaging things and he wasn't really interested in her. Sara's lack of confidence started to well up inside of her once again and she sunk back into her seat. Mr. Stone said they were watching a film and turned off the lights. Sara was tempted to look at Ethan but didn't. He seemed mad or something, sitting back in his chair with his arms folded across his chest. The film was about the life cycle of a butterfly and was extremely boring. Sara tried to think of what to say to him when the film ended, but as soon as the bell rang he was up and out of his seat and gone before she even had a change to turn her head to say a word.

Amy stopped her on the way out to her car. "What are you up to this afternoon?" she asked.

"Not much. Why?"

"We don't have practice today and a bunch of us are headed over to Jasper's to grab some food and to hang out. Do you want to come?"

"Oh," Sara said.

"Come on it will be fun, besides you said you would come out tonight for pizza anyway." Amy protested.

"Sure," Sara said, a little nervous.

"Is everything okay with you? You look a little sad or something."

"No. I mean, did I do something to Ethan Campbell?"

"What are you talking about?" Amy said.

"Well, he totally ignored me in biology today. We are lab partners and he didn't say one word to me."

"I am sure it has nothing to do with you. You know guys, they are moody sometimes. Come on, let's go have some fun," Amy said, grabbing Sara's arm and heading toward their cars.

Sara followed Amy's bright blue VW bug, very fitting to her personality. Jasper's was the local high school hangout. The smell of greasy food hit her like a shock wave as they walked inside. Big-screen TVs lined the walls, with pool tables and a jukebox in the back. Jasper's was a perfect place to hang out and waste away the afternoon. Amy and Sara joined a bunch of people from school near the back.

"So Sara, what do you like to do for fun?" Kristin asked.

"Oh, I don't know. The usual stuff I guess—hang out, go running, listen to music, shopping, yoga," she replied.

"Running, like track?" Amy asked.

"Well, I used to be on the team until last year at my old school but I kind of gave up on that when we moved here." Sara said.

"Ever think about giving the cheerleading squad a try?" Amy asked.

"Oh no, I don't think I am coordinated enough to do that," She said, shaking her head.

"Oh come on now, if you can do yoga, you can cheer," Amy said convincingly.

The other girls were trying their hardest to get Sara to try out, but she wasn't totally into it. It just wasn't something that interested her. Everyone staring at her in uniforms that barely covered parts of her body that she didn't show anyone outside the privacy of her own room. Just as she was thinking *no, thanks, to that*, Ethan and a bunch of the guys from the team walked in. Practice must have ended early. Her heart skipped a beat. Her palms got sweaty and her stomach tightened up.

"Hey guys, over here." Kristin waved, summoning them over to where the girls were sitting.

Sara pulled Amy aside and said, "Um, I think I should probably get going."

"Not a chance, just relax," she said with a smile. Sara tried to sit back and go unnoticed but Ethan saw her and came over.

"Hey Sara," he said with his warm grin. This totally confused her.

"Hi Ethan," She said, her face getting rosy.

"How's it going? How was your second day?"

"Fine, how about you?"

"Not bad. So...are you coming to the game this weekend?"

"Um, yeah. I mean Amy convinced me to come. She claims it will be a lot of fun," Sara said, trying not to sound totally weird.

"I saw your car in the lot, red '69 Mustang, it's awesome." Ethan said.

"Thanks, you drive a Mustang too?" Sara hinted, trying not to make it too obvious that she noticed these things.

"Yeah, although mine isn't as cherry as yours," he said with a smile. His eyes sparkled. Ethan took off his varsity jacket and put it on the back of the booth. He was wearing a tight navy t-shirt and faded blue jeans. His muscles flexed as he sat down in the booth.

Amy and Kristin eyed each other with a smile. Ethan never went out of his way to talk to the girls in town before. In fact, Amy hadn't seen Ethan interested in someone in a long time.

"Hey Ethan, don't you think Sara should try out for the cheerleading squad?" Amy asked him from across the table. Everyone turned and was staring at Sara now.

Ethan turned to face her and said, "Yeah, she definitely should." Sara could feel her face turning hotter by the second. She tried to change the subject to get the attention away from her. She was not used to being the center of attention and it made her even more nervous than just sitting so close to Ethan. "Are you feeling better?" Sara asked.

"Feeling better?" Ethan looked confused.

"You looked pretty bad today—like something was making you

sick or something in Biology," Sara said, trying to let him know that his coldness toward her earlier had not gone unnoticed.

"Oh that. It was nothing," Ethan said, playing it off coolly.

Someone had put Def Leppard's *Pour Some Sugar on Me* on the jukebox, and people were dancing near them in the back of the restaurant. Amy grabbed Sara's hand and pulled her to dance with the others. Sara was a little shy, but no one was paying much attention to her specifically, so she eased up and just had fun. The girls could really dance and Sara thought following their lead was fun.

Mike, Ethan, and Bobby hung back at the table watching them.

"E, get a load of them!" Mike motioned toward the dancing girls.

"Um, why are we sitting here all alone when there are some serious hotties back there needing some company?" Ethan said.

"Exactly what I was thinking," Mike said, and they got up to join the group. Mike took Amy by the arm and spun her around and started dancing close to her. Amy looked like she was enjoying herself. Ethan got close to Sara but didn't say anything, just smiled at her. They danced really close. Ethan was an awesome dancer. Sara did her best to show her flirtatious side without showing off too much. The song ended and a slow song came on. Ethan put his hand on the small of Sara's back and they continued dancing. Sara was so nervous and didn't want to say the wrong thing. She put her arms around his neck and he put his strong arms around her waist as they swayed to the beat of the music.

"You can really move," Ethan said, impressed by her dancing skills.

"You are not so bad yourself," Sara said, trying so hard to sound confident.

"Thanks, I will tell my dance teacher," Ethan said with a laugh.

"Cute."

"That is an understatement. So what do you like to do for fun?"

"You mean there is more to this town than football and hanging out watching paint dry?" Sara responded sarcastically, remembering the way he had acted toward her earlier.

"Ouch, watch it. You are dissing my home town," Ethan joked back defensively.

They finished dancing, and on the way back to the tables Sara glanced at her watch and said, "Wow, it's getting late. I should probably be getting home before my dad sends out a search party for me."

"I'll walk you to your car," Ethan said.

"Um, that's OK. I am fine, it's just outside," Sara said, grabbing her bag and heading for the door.

"Come on, I want to check out that ride of yours up close," Ethan said. Sara could feel her face getting hotter by the second. She was parked just outside the door so they didn't have to go very far.

"You know, you might just have to let me drive this sometime so I can compare it to mine," Ethan said, motioning to his car which happened to be parked next to Sara's car.

"We will see," Sara said, unlocking her door and throwing her things on the seat next to her. It was an awkward moment and she wasn't really sure what to say. "Well, bye." Sara finally said.

"Bye," Ethan said, crossing his arms and leaning on his car as he watched her get into the car and drive off.

After Sara left, Ethan went back inside and sat next to Amy. "What gives?" Amy said to him.

"What do you mean?"

"Why were you so cold toward Sara in Biology today?"

"Ughh. It's just...John Waters. He was hanging all over her at lunch today, just trying to get under my skin and something in me just wanted to pound him," Ethan said with frustration in his voice as he slammed his fist on the table.

"You have to get over that, Ethan. It was so long ago."

"I know. I just don't want him getting in the way with Sara."

"Sara is not your old girlfriend, she is different. Besides, I thought you weren't interested in her," Amy said slyly.

"I think I might be more than interested," Ethan said smirking a bit. Just then Mike came and sat down next to Amy.

"Hey there, good looking," he said.

"Hey, yourself," Amy responded, smiling.

"What are you guys chatting about?"

"Apparently Ethan isn't over the whole John Waters incident and needs to move on with his life and ask Sara out already."

"Forget him, E. I have, and he isn't worth wasting your time over. Now, I am starving. Let's eat," Mike said, summoning the waitress.

Amy got up and headed toward the jukebox to play some more music. "She's so hot," Mike said to Ethan. Ethan slapped Mike on the shoulder and shook his head. Mike Hale was a sweet guy. He was five-eleven with a typical football player build. He had black hair cut short, and dark brown eyes. Mike and Ethan were best friends and knew each other better than they knew themselves sometimes. Ethan knew Mike liked Amy but also knew that he wasn't about to make the first move without some indication that what he was feeling was mutual, because he was scared of getting hurt.

Sara headed straight home, her stomach full of butterflies and also grumbling from not eating much that day. She couldn't believe Ethan went out of his way to talk to her. She had almost forgotten completely the way he acted toward her earlier. Sara also couldn't believe the way he moved when he danced. She thought because he was a quarterback he had to be light on his feet and fast, and she also thought that he was both those things on top of being majorly smooth. She smiled, acknowledging to herself that maybe he was slightly interested in her, maybe a little more than she was ready for. She parked her car in the garage and walked in through the kitchen. Her mom had left her a plate of food on the counter as if telepathically knowing she wouldn't eat dinner and would come home ravenous. Sara micro waved the plate of food and grabbed a glass of water and headed up to her room. She could hear the television in the den so she popped her head in to tell her parents she was home. Her mom was watching television alone.

"I am home," Sara said.

"Oh honey, I didn't hear you come in."

"Where is Dad?"

"Oh, he called a while ago, said there was something he needed to take care of and not to wait dinner," Mom said.

"What are you watching?" Sara asked, sitting the plate of food down on the coffee table. Sara felt bad that her mom was sitting alone so she decided to forgo going up to her room to keep her company for a while. Sara sometimes forgot that while she left her friends behind and that was awful for her, her mom was pretty lonely too. Being new in town wasn't exactly easy on her either.

"Some miniseries on Lifetime, it's a tear-jerker," Mom replied.

"Sounds thrilling."

"Hey, how was your day?" Mom said, turning down the volume on the television.

"It was okay. I had fun tonight," Sara said, blushing at the thought of dancing with Ethan.

"So did this fun event happen to involve one of those football players you spoke about last night?" Mom asked, nudging Sara's arm. Sara and her mom had an easy relationship, one that let them talk candidly with each other.

"Yeah, but don't say anything to Dad yet. I am not even sure Ethan likes me. I mean I think he does, but this is all new for me," Sara said.

"I promise, but you have to promise me that if things do get more serious that I can meet him," Mom said.

"Deal" Sara said, picking up the plate of food and settling down into her chair.

Later that night Sara's cell phone rang. It was Amy. "What are you wearing on the field trip tomorrow?" Amy asked.

"I don't know, probably cords or something, why?"

"Do you own a skirt?"

"Sure. Why?"

"How about boots?"

"Sure, are you going to answer me?"

"I will be there in ten minutes and will explain then."

The doorbell rang exactly ten minutes later and Mom answered it. Mom let her in and Amy introduced herself. Sara called out from the top of the stairs, "Come on up" and Amy ran up the stairs.

"What is going on?" Sara asked.

"Oh my gosh, as if you didn't notice," Amy said, closing the door to the room.

"What are you talking about?"

"Ethan Campbell is totally into you," Amy gushed, moving toward Sara's closet, casually making herself at home.

Sara sat on her bed dumfounded by Amy's words. She was hoping that his attention was because he was interested, but when someone just throws those words out into the air it's another thing altogether. "I don't think so. I mean he was just being nice and everyone was talking together," Sara said, trying not to hyperventilate.

"You don't know Ethan the way I know him. I have been his friend since like kindergarten and I have never seen him act the way he is acting around you. He likes you, I can so tell. You should have seen his face when you were dancing together. So we have to get you looking irresistible tomorrow, make him drool a bit," Amy giggled.

"I don't know. I mean I am not usually one to make myself up and all," Sara said apprehensively. Not that Sara was a Plain Jane or anything, but she never really spent all that much time on the way she looked. Sara's idea of wearing makeup was usually a little mascara and lip gloss.

"That is why I am here to help you, silly." Amy said with a great big smile.

Amy raided Sara's closet and decided on a pencil denim skirt with knee high brown leather boots and a green cardigan sweater that was a little too tight for Sara's usual taste with a white camisole underneath. She helped Sara get her makeup perfect but not overly made up and used a large curling iron to put Gisele waves into Sara's unruly long blond hair. As Sara stood in front of the mirror looking at this person that was supposed to be her, waves of nausea came flooding over her. She sat down on the floor breathing deeply.

"Sara, are you alright?" Amy asked, kneeling down next to her.

"Yeah…I am…just…a little freaked out is all," Sara said between breaths.

"Hey, calm down. Listen, just be yourself, because that is what attracted Ethan in the first place and if that isn't good enough, then to hell with him, right?"

"I guess you are right," Sara said, calming down a bit. "But all this… is this me?" Sara asked her motioning to the clothes, hair, and made up look.

"Look, I was just trying to help. Maybe I went a little overboard." Amy said realizing that what she had just said really was right. Just being herself is what attracted Ethan to Sara. They toned down her look a bit and Sara began to relax again. After an hour or so they were giggling and all the anxiety that had been there earlier had disappeared.

"Okay, I will see you in the morning and don't forget just act cool and everything will work out, you'll see."

"Thanks Amy, you are really sweet."

"Hey, what are friends for? By the way in case you change your mind, tryouts for the squad are tomorrow after school. You should seriously come," Amy said,

"I don't know about that one," Sara said, but something inside her made her think twice as she said that.

Sara walked Amy to the front door and then headed back up to her room after she left and she took off the clothes that they had played dress-up in and hung them back up for the morning, hoping to not wrinkle anything. It was pretty late and Sara yawned, stretching. She wondered if she could get her makeup and hair in the morning just the way they had done it this evening. Amy made it look so easy to do. For the hell of it she packed a bag with some workout clothes and put it next to her school bag just in case she got the nerve to go to that tryout. As tired as Sara was, she tossed and turned in bed again. She tried catching up on her reading, and ended up watching infomercials before falling into a deep sleep.

Chapter 2

Morning came before she knew it after another mostly sleepless night. She woke up early, showered, and got ready for school. She came downstairs looking strikingly beautiful and Mom was nearly speechless. The last time Sara looked this good she was in a dance school recital at age ten, wearing a tutu.

"Wow, you look great."

"Thanks, Mom."

"Have a good day honey. Will you be home for dinner?"

"Not sure, I will call and let you know," Sara said, grabbing her keys and heading out the door. She pulled into what had now become her parking spot at the end of the lot, gave herself a once-over in the rearview mirror, took a deep breath, and got out of the sanctuary of her car.

Amy met her in the parking lot for moral support with Kristin also looking gorgeous—but then again they always looked put-together. Apparently, Sara looked better than she thought because a few guys gathered near them following closely as they walked toward the buses. The guys were staring like they had never seen someone dress up before.

"Have you seen Ethan yet today?" Kristin asked Sara hopefully.

"No, but please don't make me nervous or I may throw up," Sara said, feeling the butterflies churning in her stomach.

They walked toward the crowd waiting to get on the buses to go to the local greenhouse for the biology field trip, Sara self-consciously wishing she had grabbed her jacket, and waited together. The air was chilly and Sara felt the cold the instant the wind picked up. She shivered a bit as the wind tossed her hair to one side.

Everyone was busy talking about the game and the after party. Mike and Ethan came toward the group together. Ethan took one look at Sara and felt the instantly blood rush to his head.

"Damn, man," Mike said to Ethan under his breath. Ethan just stared from a distance.

"Did you see Sara?" Bobby said to them as they headed toward the buses.

Ethan gave him a nudge in the ribs and kept walking. Everyone got on the buses. Sara grabbed the empty seat across from Amy and Kristin. Ethan came up the steps and saw her sitting alone and sat down beside her. "Hey," he said to her with a big smile on his face.

"Hey, yourself," Sara said, trying to sound confident. She noted to herself that the one thing that was so intriguing to her was that Ethan was always smiling. Like he was happy all the time, unlike most teenagers.

"Looking good today," he said looking her over head to toe.

"Thanks, you don't look so bad yourself."

"Yeah well, I try," he said jokingly. He did look good. Ethan was wearing a black fitted shirt that showed off his muscles under his varsity jacket and a pair of jeans that fit him as if were made for him.

"I just wish I had grabbed a jacket, it's a little chilly today," Sara said trying to warm her hands.

Amy leaned across the seat and interrupted their conversation, "Hey, what time is everyone getting to Mike's lake house after the game?"

"The party should be in full swing around seven, but everyone is welcome right after the game. There will be plenty of beer to go around,"

Mike said. A burst of cheers from in the back of the bus greeted this announcement.

"Will you be there?" Ethan asked.

"Amy and I are going together."

"Cool," he said, and turned back to his conversation with the guys.

The buses got going and headed toward the greenhouse. Sara's palms were sweating sitting so close to Ethan. The waves of nervous energy were taking over and she was afraid to speak. Amy leaned across the aisle and mouthed the word "breathe" to her. She took a deep breath, and let it out slowly, closing her eyes. The bus was loud and everyone was on high gear about the game on Saturday. Ethan didn't have much to say to her directly; although occasionally he would glance at her with his incredible smile. Sara was starting to feel self-doubting again, like maybe she was crazy for thinking he might like her. After all, she had only known him a few days, and what could make her so interesting? Ethan could have any girl in this town he wanted. He was popular, good looking, and from the few conversations they had, he was easy to talk to. What would he find her fascinating for? Sara stared out the window watching the trees pass and got lost in her thoughts. They got to their destination a few minutes later and everyone piled off the buses. Sara joined Amy and Kristin toward the front of the group while the guys hung toward the back.

"Well, what did he think?" Amy said.

"He didn't say much actually and I was too busy trying not to throw up from nervousness. He smells incredible today. I mean his cologne was making my head spin." Amy and Kristin laughed. "I don't know Amy, I mean, do you really think he is interested in me?"

"Just breathe, OK, and remember what I said last night about just being yourself."

They followed their class through the greenhouse and tried to pay attention to everything the tour guide was saying in case of a pop quiz on this stuff later.

"Dude, Sara is totally hot. Did you check out those boots?" Mike said to Ethan.

"She could ride me like a pony in those," Bobby said.

"You need to be getting some of that sweetness," Sam said.

"Sam, I wouldn't say that so loud or Kristin might overhear you and get jealous," Ethan said.

"No worries there my friend."

"Oh really, would you like me to point out the last time you had wandering eyes and how long you had to kiss her butt to make up for it?" Ethan said smugly.

"You in to her, E?" Bobby asked Ethan.

"Let's just say I feel a sweet tooth coming on," Ethan replied, and Mike threw his arm around his shoulder. With that, Ethan caught up to where the girls were and started walking closely next to Sara.

"Hey Sara." He said.

Sara turned around and Ethan had pulled a flower from his backpack. "For you, sweetness," he said, handing her the flower.

Sara instantly blushed and shyly said, "Thanks." Ethan stayed close by as they walked together through the greenhouse. Amy and Kristin smiled, encouraging her to keep talking, and walked on ahead of them.

"So…what have you got against Simpleton?" he asked, shoving his hands into his pockets trying to make small talk.

"Nothing, it's OK, I mean I haven't found a whole lot to do yet."

"What did you like to do in your hometown?"

"I don't know, I guess I hung around with friends, took yoga classes, went running…"

"So you are an athlete?" he said with surprise.

"Well, I used to be, but moving here kind of changed a few things for me. So I guess to answer your question, not exactly, I just like to take care of myself."

"I can see that," he said, flirting with her again. Sara put the flower to her face and smelled it. "You know… Amy is right, you should try out for the squad. You sure do look like you could handle it," he said with that smile that made Sara melt inside. He was definitely flirting with her. They stopped to look at some plants that Mr. Stone was lecturing about.

"We will see," Sara answered flirtatiously, and continued walking ahead of him. Ethan caught up to her again fast. "Have you lived here your whole life?" She asked him.

"Yep, my parents are from here as well. They were high school sweethearts."

"Really? You don't hear that so much anymore. Do you have any brothers or sisters?"

"No, just me. My father wants me to follow in his footsteps and take over the family business after med school," he sounded unsure of himself.

"Is that what you want?"

"I don't know. But who knows what I want now anyway. I would be happy just to get a scholarship and spend the next four years figuring out what to do with my life," he said, ending the subject abruptly. They walked to the end of the greenhouse, completing the tour, and then out toward the buses. They all piled in and Amy sat with Sara on the way back. Kristin and Sam sat together.

"Hey, what do you think of Mike?" Amy asked quietly, looking back toward him.

"Why?"

"I think he's cute and he seems to be giving me the vibe like it's mutual, or at least that is what I am picking up on."

"Go for it, I mean you are head cheerleader, gorgeous, and any guy would want you, seriously," Sara said.

"On top of being totally hot and on the team, his parents are loaded. Just wait until you see his house Saturday night."

"He doesn't seem the snobbish type to me though."

"He isn't, his family comes from old money or something, but I don't care about that really. He is totally gorgeous."

"I'd say go for it just because he is hot!" Sara laughed.

"So what did you and Ethan chat about?"

Sara glanced over her shoulder at him; he was deep in conversation with the guys in the back of the bus. "Mostly small talk," Sara replied, looking down at the flower he had given her.

They arrived back at the school and Sara headed toward her car thinking she was crazy for even considering trying out for the cheerleading squad. Amy had no clue what Sara was about to do.

Ethan stopped Amy as she was getting her bag out of her car and said, "What's Sara's number?"

Amy gladly told him her cell number and said, "Be nice, she is shy."

"Have you ever known me not to be nice?"

"Ethan, I am serious. She is a sweet person, just take it slowly with her. I have to ask you something between us, OK?" Amy said, turning her back so that no one could see what she was saying to him.

"What's up?"

"Do you think Mike likes me?"

"Why? Are you into my boy?"

"I just don't want to make a fool out of myself if he isn't interested."

"Amy, I have known you practically all my life and you have never looked like a fool. Do you want me to say something to Mike for you?"

"Please don't tell him I told you."

"Amy, you know you can trust me."

Sara grabbed her bag and headed back toward Ethan and Amy. Ethan turned his back and the guys all headed to practice. Saturday was the biggest game of the season for them and they had to be the best. Coach lectured them about their plays, but kept the practice pretty short because he didn't want to exhaust them before the big game. He wanted them mentally focused, not exhausted to the point they wouldn't be on top of their game.

Meanwhile, Amy saw Sara's bag and said, "Are you going to try out?"

"Let's just say something changed my mind today. But no special treatment, okay?"

Amy and Kristin were so excited they practically dragged Sara into the gym. Tryouts were a lot harder than Sara had imagined they would be. She hadn't worked out that hard in a long time and her muscles were screaming by the time it was over. She had to get more yoga stretches in if she was going to be serious about this cheerleading thing. Sara managed to keep up and thought she did a pretty good job with the early part of the routine. Football practice ended earlier than tryouts and the guys were headed toward the locker room to shower up when they stopped to watch. Sara got nervous when she noticed them and didn't think she could finish the routine, which included quite a few flips, hand springs, and high jumps ending in a full split. Ethan and Mike were in a trance watching the new recruits trying out; mostly Ethan was staring at Sara. She tried to concentrate on her balance and not on the fact that he was staring right at her. Sara had opted for a triangle sports bra top and low-rise yoga pants thinking she would be able to move around easier without a bunch of clothes getting in my way, but now that they were staring she wished she had something else covering her body.

"Check out the body on Sara, E," Mike said to Ethan.

"Can't take my eyes off of her," Ethan responded as if in a trance.

Mike said to Ethan, "So did you get Sara's number from Amy?"

"Yeah," Ethan turned his attention back to Mike. "Hey, speaking of Amy, I noticed she was flirting with you pretty hardcore the other day."

"I know man, she is super hot. Did you see those little shorts she is wearing? Do you think she is into me?"

"Isn't it obvious man? You should ask her out."

"She is coming to the party Saturday night; maybe we will see what happens then," Mike said, snapping his helmet at Ethan.

"Just be nice to her man or I'll have to beat your ass. She is my friend."

"Hey, I wouldn't do anything you wouldn't do," Mike said, as he headed toward the locker room to shower. Ethan and Mike quickly showered, grabbed their things and headed out to the gym where tryouts were wrapping up. Sara was a mess, sweating with her unruly heap of hair up in a ponytail, trying to catch her breath. The tryout results would be in by Monday and since there weren't that many people trying out (mostly freshman) she thought that she had a pretty good chance of making the squad. Sara pulled on her favorite Harvard sweatshirt and said her goodbyes to Amy and Kristin and made her way wearily toward the parking lot. Mike stopped to talk with Amy, and Ethan followed Sara out. He held the door for her and said, "You looked pretty good out there today."

Sara's face was flush from tryouts so she didn't mind the extra blushing at the moment. She replied, "Um, thanks. It was a lot harder than I imagined it would be. I give Amy credit for staying so fit."

"Oh, I think you will fit right in."

They walked toward their cars together and Sara's heart was racing being so close to him.

"Well, I gotta run. See you and good luck Saturday," Sara said, opening her car door and tossing her bag inside.

"Not if I see you first," Ethan said, tapping the hood of her car and walking away with a huge grin on his face. Sara drove away, exhausted from the tryouts and eager to get home to tell someone about her exciting day.

Back in the parking lot Ethan was putting his gear in his car when Bobby and Sam approached him.

"Hey E, let me ask you something?" Bobby said.

"What's up?"

"I was just wondering if you were going to ask Sara out?"

"Why?" Ethan said.

"Dude, are you blind? She is smoking hot and if you aren't interested I am."

"Look man, Sara is off the market as far as anyone is concerned but me."

"Duly noted. See ya later man," Bobby sounded disappointed as he got into Sam's car.

Mike came toward Ethan as he stood by his car. He tapped on the roof.

"What was that all about?" Mike asked.

"Just making it clear that Sara is off limits."

"Mmmhmm, that's my boy. Now let's go get some food, I am starving."

Chapter 3

Later that night after keeping her mom company, Sara lay on her bed thinking. Her dad was working late again, which was unusual since they had moved to Simpleton. Her suspicions were up that something bad had happened; maybe a car accident or possibly worse. Being the daughter of a police officer, especially the chief of police, she grew up with a inherited tendency for questioning. Simpleton was a safe town, nothing out of the ordinary happened here, which is why her dad had taken the job and chose to move his family here. Sara didn't think where she had grown up was all that dangerous, but her dad was comforted by the fact that this was a town where everyone knew everyone and crime was minimal. There was a knock on Sara's bedroom door.

"Sara honey," Mom said.

"Come in, Mom. Is everything all right? Is Dad OK?"

"He is fine. He called a little while ago to say he would be late. Sara, did you know a girl from school named Kim Randall?"

"No. Why?"

"Well, apparently she has gone missing. Your dad is out with a search party looking for her now."

"Missing? Like she ran away?"

"He didn't say, but I am sure he doesn't know much yet. If you hear anything at school, please be sure to let your father know."

"Sure Mom. Good night."

After her mom closed the door behind her, Sara had picked up her cell to call Amy and wish her luck tomorrow when it rang in her hand.

"Hello" Sara said, not knowing the number that flashed on caller ID.

"Sara. Hey, it's Ethan." Her jaw dropped at the sound of his voice. She couldn't believe he was calling her.

"Um, hey," Sara replied, trying not to sound nervous.

"Did I catch you at a bad time?"

"No, um... not at all. What's up?" she asked him, trying not to sound like a dork and fidgeting with her hair.

"I was trying to wind down, you know, long day and all but I couldn't stop thinking about you and thought what better way to relax than talk to you?" he said with an air of confidence in his voice.

"Seriously?" Sara responded, shocked by his answer.

"Why wouldn't I want to talk to you?"

"Um, I don't know," Sara said, taking a seat on her overstuffed chair.

"So what did you think of that field trip today? Pretty lame stuff, huh?"

"I don't know; it wasn't all that bad. At least we got out of classes today."

"True."

"So are you nervous about the game on Saturday?" Sara asked, trying to make small talk. She continued to twirl her hair around the index finger of her left hand.

"I guess, but we are really tight. I mean practice is solid and the team is really working hard this year. I think we could go all the way to state champs, but that is my wishful thinking."

"My dad said he heard you guys were pretty good. I guess I will find out on Saturday."

"So, do you think you made the squad?"

"Not sure. It's not a big deal if I didn't. It isn't like I was dreaming of being a cheerleader all my life or anything."

"Why did you end up trying out then?"

Sara's face grew hot just thinking of the answer, *you of course*, but she would never say that so she ended up saying, "I wanted to see if I was up to the challenge."

"Challenge huh. So, tell me more about yourself."

"There isn't much to tell. You know my Dad is the police chief, we just moved here, I drive a Mustang."

"I mean tell me what are you into, what kind of music are you into, what's your favorite color, etc."

"I love the Dave Matthews Band," Sara offered.

"They are totally awesome, ever see them in concert?"

"Like about 10 times in the last few years. Sorry, I must sound like a total dork," Sara said without even thinking.

Ethan laughed. "You couldn't be a dork if you tried."

"You haven't known me long enough yet. My older brother used to call me that when I was little—sort of his pet name for me."

"Brother? Where is he now?"

"Brian is at Harvard, he is pre-med. That is where I want to go after high school."

"Harvard, wow really? That is quite an ambition."

"Brian and I always dreamed of going to Harvard growing up. He is already living my dream now so I am quite jealous of him. Moving here to Simpleton has been really hard on me and he has been very supportive. Most of my friends back home didn't understand why we had to move, so it's been kind of lonely since I have moved here. Sorry, I tend to babble a bit. That is probably way too much information," Sara said.

"No, please don't stop talking. I told you I am a good listener."

"I want to be an attorney and what better place to go than Harvard, right?"

"Sounds like you are close to your brother?"

"Yes, but we don't see each other much since he went away to school. Mostly holidays and summer break."

"I bet that is hard on you. You and Amy hit it off pretty well."

"Yeah, Amy is great but you already know that don't you?"

"We have known each other forever I guess. So, you are coming to the game on Saturday, right?" Ethan said, changing the subject.

"Yeah, I'll be there," Sara said, smiling.

"How will I know?"

"I'll be in the top row of the bleachers wearing a red wool coat. You can't miss me."

"Red huh, is that your favorite color?"

"How did you guess?"

"Red coat, red mustang…"

"Right, I guess I hadn't thought about it that way. I am pretty predictable I guess," Sara laughed at the obvious.

"I would have to say you have been anything but predictable."

Sara thought it was easy talking to him when he wasn't looking her in the eye. They talked about school, football, movies, and mutual friends. The conversation flowed easily like they had known each other forever. They had so much in common. After well over an hour Ethan said "Well, I guess I had better get going—it's getting pretty late. See you tomorrow?"

"Sure."

"'Night Sara."

Sara thought to herself *Oh my gosh* in disbelief that Ethan had called her. She forgot all about calling Amy. Her face was flushed and her mind was spinning from talking to Ethan. He was so easy to talk to. Sara tried to picture him talking to her, what he was wearing, what he was doing. She couldn't believe the effect he had over her. Sara had a huge crush on him. This wasn't like her; she wasn't the type of girl that just fell head over heels in love with a guy. She had never really had a serious boyfriend before. Sara thought, *Wait, I am getting way ahead of myself. I'm not even certain that Ethan likes me in that way. He could just be acting totally nice toward me because he wants to be friends for all I know. I can't help myself though. He is insanely gorgeous and he is showing interest in me.*

She showered, letting the hot water run over her tired and achy muscles. After drying her hair and slipping into her favorite PJs she climbed into bed thinking *How am I ever going to fall asleep now?* Despite her racing thoughts though, it wasn't hard to fall asleep after all the physical activity from events of the day. She quickly fell into a deep sleep and slept soundly until morning.

Chapter 4

Saturday—game day—came before Sara knew it. The sun was shining and it was crisply cold; perfect football weather. The game started at 3:30 and pretty much the entire town would be there from what Sara gathered between people talking at school and the local news coverage. Her dad was still at work pulling a 24-hour shift searching for the missing girl. Sara thought the girl's parents must be worried sick by now. She knew her dad wouldn't rest until she was found. Trying to lift her mood, Sara showered and got ready for the game.

"So what are you up to today?" Sara asked her mom.

"Oh, laundry, house cleaning, the usual." Sara suddenly felt sad that her mom didn't really have any friends here in Simpleton. She made a mental note to do something with her tomorrow.

"Any word from Dad?"

"Nothing yet. I think I will bring him lunch, I am sure he is exhausted and starving."

"Well, I don't want to be late. Tell him I said Hey," Sara said, grabbing her red coat and heading out to the high school. As she got closer to the school, Sara was startled at the mass of people crowing the streets and parking lot. After circling the block a few times she managed to find an empty space next to a large oak tree and parked. She had not anticipated anything like what she was seeing. Sara was not much of a crowd person so this was going to be an interesting afternoon. She spotted a few people she recognized from school and headed in that general direction toward the football field.

"Hey, Sara," John Waters said, stepping in front of her. Sara almost fell into him as he cut her off.

"Hi," she said, a little shocked at his surprise entrance.

"So, you got suckered into watching the game?" John said sarcastically.

"I am giving it the benefit of the doubt."

"You want to blow this game and get the hell out of here, go have some real fun?"

"Uh, thanks for the invitation, but I think I am going to watch the game," Sara replied, taken off guard by John's forwardness.

"Maybe another time then?"

"Um… maybe. Well, I had better get going if I want to see the kickoff," Sara said and kept walking toward the bleachers. She didn't look back, but got a weird feeling in the pit of her stomach. At her old school, guys weren't exactly knocking down the door to ask her out. In fact, Sara hadn't really dated much at all. She wondered if being new and people not really knowing much about her made her more interesting. Sara had always thought of herself as a quiet, boring person. She wasn't used to the attention, but thought it was flattering. Sara said hello to some fellow classmates and they invited her to sit with them in the stands. Staying true to her word, she made her way to the top of the bleachers so that Ethan would see her.

The cheerleading squad had entered the field area and was working hard to get the crowd on its feet. If you closed your eyes and listened you could imagine yourself at a professional football game by the roar of the crowd. Simpleton really supported its high school football team. Down on the sidelines, Amy and Kristen were in full uniform and looked as though they might be freezing their butts off. The idea that Sara might become a cheerleader flashed through her head momentarily and she quickly stashed that thought away. *No reason to worry about that just yet*, Sara thought to herself, shaking her head. Simpleton High's team ran onto the field and the game was under way in no time. Sara couldn't believe how exciting it was watching everyone get so into supporting her high school. The guys were playing so hard to win. Ethan threw three touchdowns in the first half of the game and Simpleton High was winning as the game went into halftime. It was hard not to get into the game with such an energetic crowd of people. Sara found herself cheering and clapping as the game broke for half time. As the guys were leaving the field Sara noticed Ethan take off his helmet, look up into the stands, and wink at her. Sara thought, *Was he really winking at me or at someone else standing up here freezing her butt off?* A warming sensation ran through her and her cheeks flushed but luckily it was so cold that no one seemed to notice.

Sara ran down to say hello to Amy and the girls and wish them luck in the second half. The team was psyched and determined to win. The day was flying by and before she knew it there was less than a minute left in the game and Simpleton High was down by one field goal. The team looked tired and they sure did play their hearts out. The referee blew his whistle signaling the end of the game just as Ethan threw the ball in a last-ditch effort to score and Mike completed the pass with the winning touchdown. The crowd went wild storming the field and lifting the players off their feet. Everyone was cheering and celebrating. It was incredibly exciting and yet a bit too close for comfort for Sara so she just hung out away from it all taking it all in.

After waiting for several minutes, the crowd began to thin and she decided to head back toward where she parked her car. She noticed her dad's patrol car in the parking lot and ventured over to see him.

"Hey honey, did you enjoy the game?" Dad asked, looking tired.

"It was actually a lot of fun. Did you get to see any of it?"

"No, I am afraid not. Just got here to do a little crowd control, not that I think anything bad is going to happen."

"Any news on that missing girl?"

"No, but don't worry we have all our available units out searching."

"Do you think she ran away?"

"Honey, you know I can't discuss an open investigation with you but at this point we don't think so and let's leave it at that." Sara, hurt a bit by his sharp response, thought *he must be tired*. It wasn't like she was trying to pry information out of him; she was just asking a simple question. "Will you be home for dinner tonight?" he asked, changing the subject.

"No, some of the girls and I are going to a party and we will grab something before then."

"Where is this party?"

"Dad, come on. You said yourself Simpleton is a safe town."

"You're right. Don't be too late and please be safe."

"Don't worry, Dad," Sara said, waving goodbye to him as she made her way toward where Amy and Kristen were congregating with the other cheerleaders.

"That was totally awesome," Sara said, approaching them.

"I knew you would have a good time," Amy said while jumping up and down, trying to stay warm.

"Hey, let's go back to my house and we can get ready for the party there. We can all ride together from there," Kristen suggested.

"Sounds good to me. I'll follow you," Sara said, heading toward her car.

The streets were crowded with spectators as Sara eased out of her parking spot. She followed them back to Kristen's house and parked her car along the street. The girls headed into the house and up to Kristen's room to warm up and change. Just then Sara's cell phone rang in her pocket.

"Hello," she answered the call, after glancing at the caller ID's unhelpful "unknown caller." No one responded, just heavy breathing. "Hello," Sara said again. Still no response so she ended the call.

"Who was it?" Amy asked, changing out of her uniform.

"No idea, just heavy breathing on the other end."

Sara was wearing her favorite jeans and a black sweater under her red coat. The girls changed into similar attire and finished primping in no time at all. Sara wished she had brought her gloves, but couldn't do much about it now. Amy helped her fix her hair which she had been wearing up in a ponytail all day. She said it looked "hot" down and flowing with soft waves so Sara let down her hair and worked some styling cream into her long locks to hold it in place.

"So I know we are supposed to wait until Monday to share the news, but we couldn't wait," Amy said to Sara.

"You made the squad, congratulations! We are going to have so much fun this year," Kristen said.

"Are you serious? I made the squad!" Sara said in shock.

"Of course you did. You were totally awesome; those freshmen had some serious competition next to you this year," Amy said.

"Now you will really get to know Ethan better. We go to some of the away games with them and practice every day too," Kristen said, fixing her hair.

"Are we ready?" Amy asked, pulling on her coat.

"Ready as I will ever be," Sara said, getting that nervous feeling in her stomach again.

"I am going to ask Mike out tonight," Amy said abruptly, checking her lipstick in the mirror. Kristen and Sara looked at her in surprise. "Well, I am tired of waiting on him to make the first move."

"I think Sam is going to ask me to Homecoming tonight," Kristen said. Kristen and Sam had been dating now for a few weeks and things seem to be going well between them. Sam Donahue was a nice guy, a bit arrogant toward most people but he treated Kristin like a princess and Sara thought that was what was important. Sam was 5'10" with brown hair and blue eyes. He was cute in a Matt Damon-ish sort of way but not Sara's type. She was happy for Amy and Kristen. They were both smart, beautiful girls and she was incredibly lucky to have met them. The girls headed out to Amy's car. Sara thought, *I hope I don't do anything stupid tonight and embarrass myself in front of Ethan.*

The drive out to Mike's lake house seemed longer than it really was in the dark. The girls chatted about guys and all the things Sara was going to need to know about the squad. Practice was every day after school and they cheered mostly home games with the exception of a few away games. They only went on one overnight trip with the guys. It was a little intense when they were telling Sara all the details, but it couldn't hurt her college resume and she was meeting such great people being so involved she swallowed back her fears and tried to sound positive about what she was getting into. School was Sara's priority this year—or at least that is what she was trying to convince herself at the moment—and if she could manage keep up her grades with the cheerleading thing then she would just quit. Besides, one more extracurricular activity on her college application couldn't hurt.

The leaves were beginning to fall and the night was cold and crisp. As they approached the house, Amy drove down a long gravel driveway toward the most beautiful log cabin tucked beside the lake. The moon was full and reflected off the water like a mirror. It couldn't have been a more serene setting. The party was in full swing when they arrived. People were everywhere. Someone had set a bonfire down by the water. Some people were roasting marshmallows and hotdogs. There were coolers of beer everywhere you looked. Sara wasn't much into drinking—it made her feel horrible and wasn't really her idea of fun. Sara and her brother had gotten drunk when she was fourteen drinking champagne at her parent's annual holiday get-together, and that was the last time she had ever touched anything alcoholic. After a horrible hangover the next day on top of being grounded for a week, she knew drinking wasn't for her.

Down by the fire, the guys from the team were all wearing their jerseys with their names on their backs so it was easy to see at a glance who was there. Sara looked around but didn't see Mike or Ethan just yet. Sam and Bobby were down by the fire and Kristen went to join them. Amy and Sara stood chatting with a few people from school; it was like the game all over again. Sara's back was to the house so she didn't see Ethan come up behind her as she stood chatting with Amy. He reached around and covered her eyes startling her.

"Guess who?"

"Hmmm, Brad Pitt," Sara said with a laugh. Ethan removed his hand and she turned around to face him.

"I told you I was betting the game on you being there today. So thanks for showing up," he said with a bright smile.

"No problem, it was my pleasure."

"Been here long?"

"Not too long. Sure looks like a lot of people came to celebrate your win today."

Ethan looked even better than earlier today when he was all roughed up and sweaty. He was wearing his varsity jacket and had his hands in his pockets to stay warm.

"Well not my win, the team really won."

"Um, I was there and it was pretty obvious you and Mike were the reason we won today." Ethan took a sip of beer, plainly embarrassed.

"You're not drinking?" Ethan asked, tipping his bottle toward her.

"No, alcohol is not my friend," Sara said with a laugh.

"You will have to fill me in on that one sometime."

"This place is gorgeous," Sara said, changing the subject.

"I know—you should see it during the day. Mike's family has lived here for generations. I think it was his grandfather's summer home when he was a kid," Ethan said. They stepped closer to the fire and Amy handed Sara a toasted marshmallow. It was sticky and warm but tasted good. Ethan went over to chat with Mike and Sam.

"Did you hear, Sara made the squad?" Sam said to the guys.

"No, but with a body like that I am not surprised. Our cheerleaders are the hottest in the state," Mike said, slapping Ethan's hand. Ethan took another drink from his beer. He glanced over to where Sara was standing.

"Just look at those lips and the way Amy licks her fingers eating that marshmallow. Oooh, I want to be those fingers," Mike joked.

"Come on, lover boy lets go talk to them before someone else does," Ethan pulled him by the arm back toward the fire.

"So did you talk to Mike yet?" Sara asked Amy as she was licking the sticky marshmallow off of her fingers.

"No, he has been pretty occupied since we got here, but the night is still young," she said sounding confident. Kristen and Sam were headed up toward the house. Amy spied them and nodded her head significantly. "I wonder what is about to happen there? Hope she doesn't do anything I wouldn't do," Amy said.

They laughed at their wicked thoughts as Ethan came back to join them and said, "Okay what's so funny?"

"Um, that is need to know information and you don't need to know," Amy said, and stuck her tongue out at him.

Ethan laughed at her and said to Sara, "Do you want to go for a walk down to the dock?"

"Sure," Sara said, looking wide-eyed at Amy for courage.

Just then Mike came over to join them. Amy took the opportunity to talk to him. "Great party, as usual."

"Thanks, it helps that it's more of a victory party and we have something to celebrate. You want a beer?" Mike said, offering Amy a bottle.

"No thanks, I'm driving. So, Mike, I was just wondering something."

"Oh yeah, like what?" he said, taking a drink.

"Like when are you going to ask me out?" Amy said fearlessly. Sara wished she had her confidence. Mike had a huge grin on his face. He stepped closer to Amy and kissed her on the lips.

Shocked, Amy pulled back and said, "You didn't answer my question."

Mike put his arms around her waist and said, "I was waiting for you to ask me." He kissed her again and that's when Ethan and Sara took their cue to head away from the fire and the celebrating and down toward the gazebo at the end of the dock. It was the most picturesque night Sara could have ever imagined. The water sparkled like diamonds in the moonlight. The temperature had dropped and you could see your breath in the night air. They sat down on one of the benches circling the gazebo.

"I can't get over how amazing this place is," Sara said to him, looking out over the water. Ethan was quiet and Sara was nervous so she started just randomly talking. "They look good together, Amy and Mike."

"Yeah," was all he said as he looked out over the water. Sara shivered a little and wrapped her arms around her body to keep warm. "Are you cold?" Ethan asked, noticing her posture.

"A little, I guess I should have worn something a bit warmer. It sure got cold fast," she said, standing and rubbing her hands together for warmth. Before Sara knew it, Ethan stepped toward her and put his arms around her body holding her close to his chest. Sara was so nervous she could have screamed at that moment. She hoped she didn't pass out from being so close to him.

"How's that?" Ethan asked.

"Much better, thanks." An awkward silence. "You played really awesome today. Although I am not a diehard football fanatic, I did have a good time," she said, looking up at him. He smelled fantastic—like spices and sandalwood. Sara's head was swirling.

"I'll have you converted in no time," he said, smiling and only adding to her dizziness.

"We will see," Sara said.

"Has anyone ever told you that you are really beautiful?" Ethan said to her, pushing a strand of hair off her shoulder.

"Not anyone that really mattered," she answered, blushing and looking down. Ethan softly lifted her chin with his fingertip so he could look at her face.

"So I matter, huh?"

Sara didn't know what to say to his question. She just bit her lower lip and waited for him to say something. "So, do you have plans tomorrow?" Ethan finally asked.

"I don't think so."

"Well, you do now," Ethan said, pulling her in closer to him.

"Oh really!" Sara said, snuggling closer to him. They stood there holding each other for a while in the moonlight. Sara wanted Ethan to kiss her but was so afraid she wouldn't be a good enough kisser to him. She looked at her watch, it was getting pretty late and she didn't want the night to end. “It’s getting pretty late; I hope Amy and Kristen don’t leave without me.”

“I can always give you a ride if you need one,” Ethan said.

“Thanks, but I have a rule never to ride with anyone that has been drinking. I should probably go back with them since we came together,” Sara said.

Ethan let go of her and said, “Come on, let’s go back to the fire”. They headed back toward the bonfire. By this time Mike and Amy were seriously making out, oblivious to everyone around them. Kristen and Sam were headed back toward the fire from the house hand in hand.

“We should probably get going,” Sara said to them.

“I’ll walk you to Amy’s car,” Ethan said motioning in that direction. Amy was saying goodnight to Mike and Sam was about to kiss Kristen when there was a loud scream from the woods.

“What the hell was that?” Mike said. The screaming got louder and everyone got quiet and then went running toward where they heard the screaming. Some of the guys on the team were playing flash light tag when someone tripped over what they thought was a log. Only it wasn’t a log. Sara saw it was the missing girl, Kim. She was dead. Her clothes were missing and she was pretty beat up. Her body looked unreal in the moonlight, like a mannequin or something. Sara turned her head and gasped into Ethan’s chest. Ethan’s face went white like a ghost and he put his arm around Sara, shielding her from the horrific site.

Instinctively Sara pulled her cell phone from her pocket and called her father. People were freaking out, crying, and running back toward the house. Amy was crying and Mike was holding her. Ethan stayed by Sara’s side holding her hand tightly until her dad arrived about thirty minutes later with backup. Crime scene investigators had also arrived with the state police and the medical examiner’s office. Everyone at the party was questioned but no one seemed to know anything. It seemed like hours later when everyone was allowed to leave. Sara’s dad told her to go straight home and she knew that she was in for it that night. Sara thought to herself that she hadn’t done anything wrong, but she was sure it didn’t look good that the Chief’s daughter was at an unsupervised party where alcohol was being served to underage kids, not to mention where the body of the missing girl was found. Sara hoped she hadn't screwed things up for her dad. She and Ethan walked toward the cars to leave the scene of this horrible crime with the vision of that dead girl burned into their brains. Ethan asked, "Do you want to ride with me?"

"Um, I think I had better go with the girls, my car is at Kristen's house," Sara said with some disappointment.

"I will get you there safely, I am totally sober now," Ethan said.

"I believe you, but I think it's best if I get home as quickly as possible," Sara said, feeling strangely guilty. A horrible thing had just happened, and here she was feeling sorry for herself for having to leave him so soon.

Amy took Kristen and Sara to her house where they recovered their own cars and drove home. Sara's mom was waiting up for her when she got home. Apparently, Dad had called and filled her in on the details.

"Sara, are you all right?" she asked as soon as Sara was through the door.

"I am fine Mom, just cold and I want to go to bed."

"Your father will want to talk to you in the morning."

Sara walked upstairs and stripped off her clothes in a pile on the floor. She climbed into the shower, letting the hot water scorch her skin. She tried to wash away the vision of that poor girl and what she must have gone through. After the water turned cold she shut off the faucet and wrapped herself in her robe. Sara wasn't sure she could sleep after all that she had been through that day but somehow her body needed it more than her brain at that point. She dreamed of Ethan. They were down by the lake in the moonlight. He was holding her like they were earlier tonight and as he kissed her a body floated by them in the water. Sara woke up screaming. It was just a dream, she told herself, but she still had trouble falling back to sleep.

Chapter 5

The next morning, Sara woke to sounds of arguing downstairs. She dressed in her brown cords and navy sweater with a white lace camisole underneath, ran a brush through her hair, and headed down to the kitchen to see what was happening.

"I don't care Molly, she shouldn't have been out there in those woods," Dad said.

"Oh, Bill, she has to make friends—and she wasn't doing anything wrong."

"That is beside the point. Do you have any idea what it looks like for her to be out there in those woods when that girl was found?"

"Hey," Sara interrupted them. "So am I grounded or what?"

"No, honey, your Dad and I are just worried. This is supposed to be a safe town and something like this puts everyone on edge."

"Dad, did you find anything at the scene? Did anyone see anything? How long had she been there? Did she suffer?" Sara hit him with a barrage of questions.

"I told you Sara, I can't talk about the case."

"Come on Dad, you have to tell us something. You were the one that moved us to this "safe" town," Sara instantly regretted that last statement.

"Just promise me you will be safe—don't go walking in those woods alone, and if you see something out of the ordinary, call me."

"I promise."

"Come on, I made breakfast. Let's at least sit down and eat it before the food gets cold," Mom said walking into the kitchen. Sara had smelled bacon and coffee brewing on the stove. Her mom set out a plate of freshly baked scones, Sara's favorite. They sat down at the table.

"So, what do you have planned today?" Sara asked her mom, trying to lighten the mood after the last conversation.

"Well, I was planning on going to town and doing a little shopping. Do you want to join me?"

"I would love to." Sara said. The doorbell rang, interrupting their conversation. It was 11:30 and they weren't expecting anyone. Sara tensed, remembering that she had made plans with Ethan last night before all the commotion. Sara felt a mix of emotions at that moment: surprise and nervousness at the prospect spending the day with Ethan and disappointment at not being able to keep her plans with her mother.

"I'll get it," Sara said, getting up from the table. Surely it couldn't be him, not after how they had left things last night. She walked to the front door and there stood Ethan on the front porch. Sara opened the door and a blast of cold air hit her in the face.

"What are you doing here?" Sara asked surprised to see him.

"Did you forget we had plans?"

"Um, yeah. I guess after all that happened last night I didn't think we would be doing much today," Sara said, a little embarrassed.

"If you aren't up for it we can always do something some another time," he said with disappointment in his voice.

"No, just…Hold on a second," Sara said and backed into the kitchen.

"Mom, I am so sorry. I forgot that I made plans today with Ethan before everything happened last night. Can we go shopping another time?"

Her mom smiled and said, "Have fun, honey."

"Wait," her father said. "I want you to bring your cell phone with you and leave it on so we can reach you."

"Always do," Sara said. She didn't feel so bad now. Sara knew that her mom understood that she would only be young once. She grabbed her leather coat and red scarf and headed toward the front door.

It was a beautiful day again, the sun was shining and the air was cold and crisp. Fall was definitely here to stay. "So where are we going?" Sara asked as they got into Ethan's car. It had that new car scent mixed with a strong leather smell, and was impeccably clean for a guy's car.

"How about a movie?"

"That sounds good to me, what's playing?

"I think there is a new Adam Sandler comedy."

They headed toward town and the movie theater. "So, your dad is cool with you about last night?" he asked.

"I think he was just as shocked as we all were. He wasn't too happy that I was out there in the woods, but I think I managed to escape being grounded."

"That's good, my parents freaked when they heard what happened," Ethan said.

"What did Mike's parents do when they found out?" Sara asked.

"Well, after they were told that a dead body was found on their property they hopped the first flight home. I think Mike is in deep trouble."

"Did you know her?" Sara asked.

Ethan was quiet for a minute before he responded. "Um... sort of. We all hung around when we were younger. She was a bit of a partier and kind of went her own way from us when we got to high school." He sounded sad as he said this.

"Oh... I can't imagine what must have happened to her. I don't know if I will ever get that image of her laying there on the ground out of my mind," Sara said, putting her head back on the headrest. They drove in comfortable silence the rest of the way into town. Sara was admiring the gorgeous weather they were having. They pulled up to the movie theater and Ethan parked. He bought two tickets to the movie and they headed inside to grab their seats. It was one of those old movie theaters with the red velvet curtains and a balcony. "I have never been inside one of these old theaters before and never sat in a balcony before now," Sara said.

It was pretty slow for a Sunday. There were only a handful of people in the entire place. Ethan smiled and took off his jacket and slung it on the back of his seat. He was wearing a black sweater and dark jeans with coca colored leather shoes. He looked like a Calvin Klein model. Sara nervously took off her jacket and rested it over the arm of the chair next to her.

"Is there anything you don't look good in?" Ethan asked, looking her up and down as she sat next to him.

"I was wondering the same thing about you," Sara said, trying to keep up the flirtatious mood.

"A Speedo bathing suit," he said with a laugh.

"Why do I doubt that?" Sara asked, looking him over head to toe. Ethan laughed again. His voice was like velvet, sultry and smooth. Sara felt like melting into the seat she was sitting in. They sat talking comfortably about their favorite movies and books for a while waiting for the show to start. Sara felt at ease with him for the first time that day. She wasn't sure why, he was still insanely gorgeous and the way he looked at her made her weak inside. Thankfully, the lights dimmed and the screen came on. They sat watching the movie and laughing at all the funny parts together. At one point Ethan reached down to Sara's left leg and took hold of her hand. His hand was warm and rough from playing football. Sara looked at him and smiled. It was obvious to her that he liked her. She hoped he would kiss her, but he didn't. She was starting to wonder if it was her—maybe she was fun to hang around with but not girlfriend material.

After the movie was over they went to Jasper's for some food. They sat in the back in a low booth that was more private so they could talk without being interrupted. Jaspers was Sunday-afternoon slow.

"Can I ask you something kind of personal?" Ethan said.

"Sure, but does it mean I have to answer?"

"Did you leave anybody special behind at your old school?"

"No. I was way too involved with school, running mostly and my friends. I mean, I guess I wasn't as interesting to most people that I had known all my life," Sara said, playing with a paper straw wrapper.

"I don't understand why you would think that. You are certainly intriguing to me," Ethan said. Sara blushed a bit. "Hey, I heard the good news about you making the squad."

"Wow, good news travels fast. Amy couldn't wait to tell me, she is more excited about it than I am actually," Sara said.

"This is a small town, remember. I guess I will be seeing you a lot more now, huh?" Ethan said.

"In those uniforms, yeah," Sara said with a laugh. Ethan grinned but didn't respond to that comment. Sara wondered what he was thinking at that moment.

"How about you, quarterback for the football team, you must be fighting the girls off with a stick?" Sara asked him.

"A baseball bat actually."

"That's not what I meant," Sara said with a shy smile.

"Nothing serious," he said while looking into her eyes. Sara could feel her face flushing. Ethan reached across the table and held her hand.

"So what do you like to do when you aren't playing football?"

"Hang out with you." Now her face was burning. He held her hand a little tighter .

"Seriously, what do you do in your free time?"

"I don't know. I help my parents at the pharmacy sometimes on the weekends when we don't have practice or a game. Mike, Sam, and I hang out some too. I guess typical stuff," Ethan said.

"What is your idea of the perfect date?" Sara asked him.

"Person or event?"

"Both."

"She has to be funny and easy to talk to. She has to be interested in her body and athletics, but most of all she has to be into Mustangs."

"Event?"

"Anyplace with you," Ethan said, softly. Sara thought for sure he would reach across the table and kiss her at that moment. At least that was what she was hoping he would do. Instead he stroked her hand across the table. Sara was getting that nervous pit in her stomach again. Suddenly, she wanted to change the subject.

"So are you worried about the Biology exam next week?"

"Not really. Science has always been a strong point for me. I guess that is why I will probably go pre-med next year because it is sort of natural for me," Ethan said.

"I thought you didn't know what you wanted to do next year?" Sara asked, thinking back to what he had said the other day.

"You know, we should study together sometime since we are lab partners. I am an expert on human anatomy," he said, ignoring her question. Sara laughed at his playful joke—at least she hoped he was joking. The flirtatious conversation went on for a while, growing that nervous pit in her stomach into a crater. She thought she might vomit at the table. *Wouldn't that make a great first date*, Sara thought.

"What about you. What is your ideal date?" Ethan asked.

"I guess it would be something special like an event where we were all dressed up or something. There would be flowers and candlelight and we could be alone together," she answered honestly, imagining that scenario with Ethan.

"Do you want to get out of here? We could go for a drive or something," he asked, feeling a bit nervous with her for the first time. Ethan thought it was incredibly beautiful the way she blushed when she was nervous and the way she played with her hair, twirling it around her fingers unconsciously.

"Yeah, that would be fun," Sara said, grateful that the were leaving the close quarters of the booth. She thought some air might do her good, help her relax a bit.

"Where do you want to go now?" Ethan asked, as they reached his car in the parking lot.

"You are from here, remember."

They got into his car and he just drove with no special destination in mind. The leaves were falling and the sun was starting to set in the sky.

Simpleton was beautiful. Ethan turned on the radio and Sara's favorite song, Peter Gabriel's *In Your Eyes* was playing.

"Oh gosh, I love this song."

"Really?"

"I listen to it when I am doing yoga, it relaxes me," Sara said, putting her head back on the seat. "What kind of music do you listen to?"

"Depends on what kind of mood I am in I guess," Ethan responded.

"My brother and I used to go to concerts every summer back home."

"What was your favorite?" Ethan asked.

"Umm that is a tough one. I hate to admit it, but Bon Jovi—they played an amazing show and sounded just like they did when I was a kid playing my cassette tape on my boom box," she said. Ethan laughed.

"So, how's the new GT compared to your classic?" Ethan asked casually.

"She purrs like a cat. Mine sounds more like a Harley ridden hard and put up wet." Sara couldn't believe she'd just said that to him.

Ethan's eyes got wide and he half grinned. "I am going to have to try that sometime."

Sara blushed and turned her head to look out the window. She was really going to have to watch what she said around him. She didn't want to give him the wrong impression or sound like an idiot either. Noticing the time she said, "I should probably get home soon before my parents send a search party for me." She'd had such a great time with him and didn't want the day to end. It was getting late though, and they did have school tomorrow.

"That's cool; I wouldn't want your Dad to get the wrong impression of me so soon." He headed the car toward her house.

As they approached her street she said, "Thanks for today; I had a great time with you."

"Me, too. Will I see you tomorrow?" he said as he pulled into the driveway. The front lights were on, which meant Sara's parents were probably in the living room watching television.

"I will be there," Sara said, reaching for the car door handle.

"Can I call you?" he asked.

"I'd like that. You have my number," Sara said as she started to get out of the car. Then she stopped herself, leaned back in, and kissed him softly on the cheek. Her lips burned at the touch of his skin. She couldn't believe her sudden boldness. She had been nervous practically all day with him, and then she just went and kissed him. "Bye," she called, and got out of the car, not looking back to see the shocked expression on his face.

Ethan backed out of the driveway and called Amy on his way home. "So, how was the date?" Amy asked him.

"Great, Sara is awesome. Now what's up with you and Mike?"

"Let's just say I got tired of him waiting to ask me out and took matters into my own hands."

"That's way cool. But if he gets rough with you I will kick his ass—you know that, right?"

"I think I can handle him," Amy said.

"I'll bet you can, " Ethan laughed.

"Did you kiss her?" Amy asked.

"Hey, a gentleman never kisses and tells. But, actually, she kissed me—on the cheek though, so I guess that doesn't count."

"She did?! Good for her."

"Listen, do you think Sara would go with me to Homecoming if I asked her, or is it too soon?"

"I think she might faint if you ask her," Amy said with a laugh.

"Seriously?"

"Not literally, but I think its worth going for. Got to run," Amy said, and hung up

Chapter 6

That next week went by in a blur for Sara. The biology exam was much harder than she had anticipated, but she managed a B. Although she had been getting more sleep than usual, Sara had been waking up feeling flu-like. Between practicing and keeping up with school projects, she was getting run down. Ethan had been another distraction for Sara, too. He would walk Sara to her locker after biology each day before they both headed to practice, and would call her each night. They would chat for several hours through homework, dinner, and sometimes watching television together over the phone. They were getting to know each other better with every conversation and Sara was becoming more at ease around him at school and in public.

Even so, it seemed like forever before Ethan finally asked Sara out on another date. They made plans to go out Saturday night after the game. Their friends were starting to get used to seeing them together so much that everyone assumed they must be dating. Were they dating? Sara often wondered, since they hadn't actually been out on a second date. It felt more like they were getting to know each other better as friends than as a couple. Sara often caught herself staring at Ethan on the football field during practice. He was so smooth in his movements, calculated and precise. No wonder he was the quarterback. People really listened to him, trusted him.

Late that Friday night after a grueling day at school and a long hard practice, Sara's cell phone rang. She rolled over and looked at the clock; it was 2:00 a.m.

"Hello," she said, still half asleep. No answer—just heavy breathing on the other end. "Ethan, is that you?" she asked. Sara looked at the caller id and saw it was an unknown caller like the previous time.

"You must have the wrong number," she said, and hung up. She got that uneasy feeling in her stomach again. She remembered the first time she got that heavy breathing call—the night the body was found. She immediately wondered if this was a sign that something bad was about to happen. The phone rang again. She jumped and swallowed hard before answering the call. This time it was Ethan calling.

"Hello."

"Did I wake you sweetness?" Ethan said.

"Not exactly. What's up?" Sara said, trying to clear what felt like stabbing needles from her throat.

"I couldn't sleep. You have been on my mind all night."

"Oh, really? What have I been doing there?"

"I don't think I should say; some things are best kept to the imagination."

"Well let me help you out with that. What are you wearing?"

"Boxers and nothing else," he replied.

"Hmm. Now my imagination is getting the best of me," Sara said softly.

"Come on, don't leave me hanging here, what are you wearing?" Ethan asked.

"Hold on a second," she said. Sara was wearing a white tank top with boy shorts. She pulled her hair out of the usual knot she slept in and let it flow freely over her shoulders. She took her phone and did her best to take a picture. She hit 'send' and a moment later heard Ethan's phone beep. "Well, what do you think? Was this what you were imagining?" she asked.

"This is way better. Except, how am I ever going to get to sleep now?"

"I am sure you will think of something. See you tomorrow" Sara said, and hung up. A few minutes later as she was just drifting off to sleep her phone beeped. Ethan had taken a picture of himself in bed in just his boxers. "Holy crap," Sara said out loud. He was gorgeous. His abs were perfect, his arms were sculpted and strong. The caption under the picture said 'Can I come over?'

She texted him back with, "If you can figure a way to get into my room without my Dad finding you, have at it."

Ethan replied, "No thanks, I value my life too much, see you tomorrow."

It was hard to believe that it had been a week since that girl was found dead in the woods. Sara's dad kept pretty quiet about it. He was working long hours and looked so tired when he was home. The newspapers were reporting that she had been raped and had died from asphyxia due to strangulation. No one in town seemed to know anything about it. Kim's family scheduled a memorial service for the following week and the papers said in lieu of flowers to make a donation to the reward for information to find her killer.

Other than what Ethan had said about her being a party girl Sara hadn't heard much else about her. She thought this was strange—someone had to know something or have seen something. *How does someone in a safe town like Simpleton just disappear and then turn up dead?*she wondered.

Saturday morning Sara woke up coughing hard. She was shivering and cold all over and most likely running a fever. Her mom suggested going to see the doctor. She knew from the way she was feeling there was no way she could go out with Ethan that night. She was disappointed at the thought, but thought maybe she might be able to still go if she got some rest. By the time she dressed and went downstairs, her Mom had made her an appointment with her doctor. Sara was feeling too ill to drive herself so her Mom went with her. It was bitterly cold outside and looked as though it might rain. Sara wrapped her scarf tightly around her throat and rested her head on the seat of Mom's car. The waiting room was empty and they didn't have to wait long before being called. The doctor ran some tests but seemed confident that it was the flu. The doctor told Sara she should get as much rest as possible and keep taking fluids. Sara was relieved that it wasn't anything serious. The drive home was short and Sara went straight up to bed where she fell asleep for several hours. When she woke, the sun had set and the sky was still heavy with clouds. Lying in the dimly lit room contemplating getting out of bed, Sara heard her phone ring. It was Brian. "Hey sis, how's it going?"

"Oh, I feel like hell."

"Are you sick or something?"

"Uh yeah, doctor says it's the flu but I think it's death for certain," Sara said, coughing.

"Not funny. How is Dad doing?"

"He is working constantly on this murder investigation. We never see him anymore."

"Any leads?"

"You know Dad; he won't talk about it."

"Typical Dad. So how come I have to hear about Mr. Wonderful from Mom?"

"Sorry Brian, I have been so busy with cheerleading and now I am sick."

"Sure, I am no good to tell all of your secrets to, now that you have a boyfriend."

"Shut up. Like you don't already know, his name is Ethan Campbell. He is the guy I was telling you about. He's the quarterback for the football team. Gorgeous. Best of all, he drives a Mustang. But no, he is not my boyfriend—or at least not yet."

"You had better tell him that if he doesn't treat my baby sister right, I am going to kick his butt when I get home for Thanksgiving."

"Okay dork. See you soon."

"Feel better. Bye."

Sara still felt horrible but realized she hadn't called Ethan yet to break their date. It was 6:30 and she knew he would be coming over soon to get her. She picked up the phone to call him.

"Hey, sweetness," Ethan answered on the first ring.

"Hey Ethan," Sara said, sounding horrible.

"Are you sick?"

"I have the flu. I am so sorry, but I won't be able to go out with you tonight or to the game tomorrow. Will you let Amy know for me?"

Disappointment obvious in his voice, Ethan asked, "Is there anything I can bring you? Chicken soup? Me?"

"No thanks. I am just going to try and rest and hopefully be fine by Monday."

"OK, get better soon and I'll see you then."

"Call me tomorrow after the game? Sorry I can't be there for good luck," Sara said with a cough.

"Don't worry about it. I'll be thinking of you—get some rest."

Sara slept deeply Saturday night and dozed through most of Sunday and woke up feeling better but still weak on Monday morning. Her skin was even paler than usual and although she had slept for almost two days, there were dark circles under her eyes. She noticed that her gums were still bleeding and little bruises had suddenly appeared on her arms and legs. She called her mom into the bathroom to show her. Her mom had a worried look on her face and said she would call the doctor to see if the test results had come back yet. She suggested that Sara stay home another day, but Sara refused. She had been cooped up in the house all weekend and wanted to go to school and see her friends. She felt like she had been a prisoner all weekend while her friends were out doing fun things together. Sara especially wanted to see Ethan. She dressed in her favorite jeans and gray cashmere sweater, with black boots and a leather jacket. She pulled her hair into a loose ponytail and grabbed her things before heading out to school.

Sara pulled her Mustang into the lot next to Amy's car. She got out and headed toward the main entrance. All of her new friends were standing inside waiting for the first bell, talking about Homecoming weekend coming up. She approached Amy and Kristen in the hall.

"Hey Sara, how are you feeling?" Kristen asked.

"Better. A little weak, but much better than I was on Friday."

"We missed you at the game this weekend. Ethan said his good luck charm was home sick and we didn't do so hot. If it wasn't for Ethan we wouldn't have won." Kristen said.

"Sorry guys, I promise to be there in the future," Sara said, feeling like she had let them down.

"Oh, come on now. It's not your fault we lost the game. It was like everyone wasn't into the game this time around," Kristen said.

Mike and Sam came toward them with the morning newspaper. "Did you hear Calley Bishop went missing this weekend?" Mike asked.

"What?" Amy said, shock in her voice as she turned to face him.

"What's going on here?" Sara asked them.

"We don't know, we thought you might know something since your Dad is Chief and all." Sam's voiced was tinged with a hint of sarcasm. Sam and Sara didn't exactly know each other that well, but he seemed to have taken a disliking to her. He was really the stereotypical jock, but he was Kristen's boyfriend so Sara felt that she had to be nice to him.

"My Dad doesn't talk about work much at home. I think you all know more than I do about what is going on in this town," Sara said, a bit defensively.

"I am scared. Maybe it isn't safe for us to be out alone anymore?" Kristen said. Sara didn't know why, but Kristen's comments made her think of those phone calls she had been getting from the heavy breather.

"Don't go jumping to conclusions," Ethan said, as he joined the group. "How are you feeling?" he asked Sara as he put his arm around her shoulder and pulled her aside so they could talk without anyone hearing.

"Better now that you are here," Sara said, perking up at his touch. She hugged him and breathed in his scent.

"I was going to ask you this weekend, but being that you were sick

I figured I would wait until I saw you in person. Would you be my date for Homecoming weekend?" Ethan said, pulling a red rose out of his jacket.

"Absolutely!" Sara said, taking the rose and hugging him again.

The bell rang and everyone went off to class. Sara was beaming inside. She forgot all about being sick as she walked to her first class.

Later that day, the cafeteria was buzzing about the girl that had gone missing. The guys were sitting at the end of the table discussing what they had heard about it. Sara was trying to listen to the conversation when Amy started talking to her. "Mike asked me to Homecoming weekend," she said happily.

"Things are going well between you two, I take it?" Sara asked her, taking a bite of an apple.

"Mike is totally awesome. He makes me feel so good. Hey, has Ethan asked you to Homecoming yet?"

"Yes, he asked me this morning actually," Sara answered. She shouldn't have felt that twinge of jealousy that Amy knew about Ethan asking her to Homecoming, but she did. Sara knew they had been good friends longer than she had known either of them, so then why did she have that feeling?

"We have to go shopping for dresses. I will call you tonight and we can make plans. Are you coming to practice today?" Amy said.

"I think I am up to it," Sara said instantly, feeling bad for her uncharitable thoughts toward Amy. Both Amy and Kristen had been nothing but nice to her since she moved to Simpleton. Sara was really excited about the dance and deep down she was happy that she was being included in the event planning by her new friends, Amy and Kristen.

On the way into the locker room Ethan stopped her and said, "Where are you off to?"

"I need to go see my dad and then home. Why?"

"No reason. Can I call you later?"

"I will be waiting to hear from you," Sara said, and hugged him before heading into the locker room. He smelled like cold air and sweat. His body was warm but his hands were cold from the chilly fall afternoon.

After practice, Sara stopped by the police station to see her dad. "Hello Sara," the receptionist said as she walked through the doors.

"Is Dad in?" Sara asked.

"Sure, hold on one second and let me see if he is available."

A moment later Sara's father was standing in the doorway. He looked stressed and exhausted. All those long hours and the lack of real evidence were getting to him and it was showing in his appearance.

"Well, to what do I owe this pleasure?"

"Dad, can we chat in your office?" Sara asked him. He led the way and they sat down in front of his large mahogany desk.

"What's up kiddo?" he said.

"Dad, I heard about that a second girl went missing this weekend. Please level with me. Is Simpleton a safe place?"

Dad sighed and said, "We haven't found her yet, but my instinct tells me these cases are connected. We are searching the lake area where the first girl was found, but nothing has turned up yet. No leads in either case," he admitted reluctantly.

"I am scared, Dad," Sara said. She wanted to mention the strange phone calls she had been getting but didn't know if they were related and didn't want her father to think she was making them up just to get more information from him.

"Don't be. I will be here to protect you and Mom."

"Dad, you have to be honest with me. Is there anyone in town that is a suspect?"

"Sara, you know I can't share that information with you."

"Dad, please don't give me that crap. Is there someone that is connected to these missing girls that we need to know about?"

"Now there is no need to worry about things like that now. Your mother is probably worried about you now, so get on home," he said, ending their conversation and dismissing Sara's concerns.

Sara left the police station angry that he couldn't be honest with her. Someone was hurting these girls and putting her and her friends in danger. Sara felt weak and sat for a moment before she started the car. Her phone rang, it was her mother.

"Sara, the doctor's office called with your blood work results."

"And, what's up?" Sara asked, suddenly nervous.

"They want you to come back for some more tests. Can you stop by there on your way home?"

"Sure, did they say why? Should I be worried, Mom?"

"No, just do what they ask, and I will see you soon."

So Sara stopped by the doctor's office and the nurse took some more blood samples from her. The doctor wouldn't say what her concerns were, just that she needed some iron and that she should try to get as much rest as possible.

Sara was kind of freaked out by the whole thing so she called Brian when she got home. There was a lot of noise in the background. "What's up?" her brother asked.

"Where are you? Sounds like a party."

"I am in the dorm, it's crazy here. People are cramming for midterms."

Sara told him everything that was going on and asked him if she should be worried. He said he would do some research and get back to her but not to worry about anything until they got the results back. "How's Dad holding up?" Brian asked.

"You know Dad."

"How's Mom? Is she making any friends yet?"

"She is fine, just worried about Dad and me. Ethan asked me to Homecoming weekend," she added happily.

"Oh really; things getting serious between you two?"

"I don't know. Brian, how long do you usually wait before you kiss a girl?"

"Why? Mr. Wonderful hasn't made a move on you yet?" he joked.

"Seriously."

"I don't know, I guess it depends on how much I like her and if the date goes well," he said. Sara got quiet and Brian said, "Keep your chin up Sara, if he is the one for you it will happen and will be worth waiting for, trust me."

"Right. Hey, thanks for looking into this for me. Call me soon," Sara said, hanging up the phone.

Sara called Amy to take her mind off of everything that was going on. "I am so happy for you," Amy said to her when they started talking about Ethan asking her to Homecoming. "We have to go shopping this weekend for dresses."

"Will you help me? I have no clue what will look good on me or how to wear my hair," Sara said.

"Absolutely, girl, you are my friend and you are going to look hot for Ethan. Who knows? You might just end up Homecoming King and Queen."

"Oh no, I would definitely faint then." Amy laughed and they made plans to go shopping with Kristen later that weekend. The guys had an away game and for once the squad didn't have to attend so it would give the girls some alone time to catch up. They hadn't spent much time together since that night at the bonfire. School and practice consumed most of their free time during the week.

Ethan called her later before Sara went to bed. "Hey sweetness," he said.

"How was practice?"

"Brutal as usual. Coach thinks we can go all the way this year so he is pushing us to our breaking point."

"Sorry to hear that."

"Do you want to go out tomorrow night? We leave Saturday morning for the game and won't be back until Sunday. I don't know if I can go all weekend without seeing you," Ethan said.

"Sure, why don't you pick me up around 7?"

"Sounds good to me. Hey are you alone?" Ethan asked.

"No, Mom is downstairs. Why?"

"Damn, I thought I could come over for a while," Ethan said, disappointed.

"See you tomorrow. 'Night, Ethan."

"Bye, sweetness."

Friday night Ethan and Sara went out for coffee. The team was leaving in the morning for the away game and wouldn't be back until late Sunday. They sat talking in overstuffed chairs at the coffee house.

"So what are you up to this weekend?" Ethan asked.

"Shopping and hanging with Amy and Kristen," Sara said, sipping a steaming latté.

"Do me a favor, be careful and don't go anywhere alone, especially at night."

"You sound like my dad, but don't worry, I will be fine," Sara said, reaching for his hand. She gave it a light squeeze, hoping to reassure him that she could take care of herself and that he didn't have anything to worry about except his game. "So are you going to win this one for me or what?" She said, changing the subject.

"We should shut them out for sure," Ethan said confidently.

"Have you started applying for college yet?"

"No, I was hoping to get a scholarship somewhere and let the decision be made for me," Ethan said.

"Oh," Sara said, surprised by his answer. Ethan always seemed so on top of things, she was sure he had someplace in mind by now.

"So, when do I get to meet your parents for real?" Ethan asked.

Sara coughed into her latte. "You want to meet my parents?"

"Well, yeah. I mean, don't you think your parents would like me?" he smiled. Sara knew they would like him and her dad would be pleased to have someone to chat about football with. But the idea of him meeting them was so formal and she wasn't sure where they were just yet.

Ethan drove her home and walked her to the door which was a first for Sara. Usually she just hopped out of the car and headed into the house, but Ethan was different.

"Will you call me when you get back Sunday night?" Sara asked him.

"Yes, if I can wait that long," he said, hugging her close.

"I know you will win, but good luck anyway," Sara said, hugging him back. She was not sure what happened at that point or who initiated it, but as they pulled apart her lips grazed his. She wouldn't call it a first kiss but it was definitely something.

"Goodnight," Sara said, and quickly went inside and closed the door. Her nerves had gotten the best of her and she thought she had just totally screwed that moment up. Maybe the reason they hadn't kissed yet was because he thought of her as more of a friend than she thought of him. Maybe Sara was the one with a huge crush and he didn't feel the same way. He did ask to meet her parents so that was something. Sara thought back to her conversation with Brian and tried to put those doubts out of her head. Ethan was with her and if he was the right one then everything would happen eventually and it would have been worth waiting for. At least that is what Sara kept telling herself.

Chapter 7

On Saturday, Amy, Kristin, and Sara drove to Derry, a larger town about thirty minutes from Simpleton. They headed straight for the large mall there to shop for dresses and spend some quality time alone. They hadn't had the opportunity to do fun girly activities since Sara had started with the squad.

"I think this one will look awesome on you," Amy said, picking up a backless red cocktail dress and handing it to Sara. She ignored the price tag because it was probably way more than she had intended to spend.

"Do you think I can pull something like this off?" She asked, holding the dress up a bit dubiously.

"I think Ethan is going to have a hard time keeping his hands off of you in this one," Kristen said.

"Plus, it's your favorite color. Go try it on," Amy urged.

Sara went into the dressing room with a completely unforgiving three way mirror. She slipped out of her clothes and into the dress. It fit perfectly, and her friends were right—it looked amazing on her. She stepped out so they could see her, and twirled around for their admiration. "Well, what do you think?"

"Sara, what happened to your back?" Amy said holding Sara's arms and pointing to the bruises on her back.

"It's nothing. My doctor is doing some tests and said I should take more iron and get some rest is all."

"Seriously, is everything okay with you?" Kristen asked.

"Look, I am fine. There is nothing to worry about," Sara said trying to sound convincing. Trying to *feel* convinced. "Don't say anything about this to Ethan, okay? Now let's find some dresses." Sara headed back into the dressing room to change and get a better look at the bruises. They were pretty small in size, maybe no larger than a quarter, but they were scattered all across her back.

Worry began to fill Sara's mind and she started to feel sick again. Was there really something wrong with her? As she was changing out of the dress her phone beeped with a text message. Figuring it was from Ethan, Sara picked up the phone. Only the message wasn't from Ethan. It was a photo of Amy, Kristen, and Sara just a few minutes ago in that very store with a caption that said 'I am watching you'. She panicked, dropping her phone on the dressing room floor and covering her mouth with her hands. Maybe they really *were* in danger. Sara hurriedly dressed and went back to where Amy and Kristin were shopping. When she saw them laughing and having a good time shopping, she decided not to say anything. Sara didn't want to over-react and freak them out too. She thought *What if it's just a sick joke or something*? She decided to keep her thoughts to herself and spent the rest of the time they were in the mall checking to see if she recognized anyone that might have sent the message. After what seemed like hours of shopping and trying on dresses, Kristen decided on a fuchsia low-cut floor-length dress while Amy went for a strapless black form fitting cocktail dress. Sara decided to go with the red dress and hoped that the bruises would be gone before the big night. The girls all found shoes and jewelry to match their dresses and then headed over to the cinema to see the new Brad Pitt movie.

In the car on the way home they got to talking about the guys.

"So how are things going with Mike?" Kristen asked.

"Girl, he makes me feel like melted butter when he kisses me. I can't help feeling sexy when I am around him," Amy said. "How about Sam, is he a good kisser?"

"Super sweet. Although sometimes I feel like he is more into me than I am into him."

"What do you mean? Is he getting too serious too fast or what?" Amy asked.

"Well, he wants to know every detail about me, but doesn't answer my questions when I ask him something important. He is kind of controlling and a little jealous too. But then other times he is sweet and understanding and things are fine and I forget about what made me feel uneasy in the first place," Kristen said.

Sara couldn't believe she was saying this about Sam. It was like she was reading her mind about how she felt about Ethan. Why she couldn't get him to talk about his future, or get a straight answer about what kind of music he likes. Maybe all guys were the same. Sara started to feel that sinking feeling in the pit of her stomach and swallowed hard.

"Okay Sara, spill it. Is Ethan a good kisser or what?" Kristen said, changing the subject.

"I wouldn't know, he hasn't kissed me yet," Sara said, trying not to sound disappointed.

"Seriously, no way? Ethan never seemed shy around other girls before," Amy said and instantly looked sheepish for saying something that insensitive out loud.

"I kissed him once on the cheek, the first night we went out and since then he hasn't attempted anything at all. Last night he was saying goodnight to me at my door and we kind of bumped faces when I went to hug him. I felt so stupid. Do you think there is something wrong with me?" Sara asked.

They both giggled, but not in a mocking way. "No way, girly," Amy said. "Ethan isn't your typical jock guy in case you hadn't noticed," she continued. "I have known him forever and he really isn't one to rush into things. He was dating this girl pretty seriously once a few years ago, but it ended badly and he really hasn't dated much since then."

"He really likes you, though," Kristin added. "He was talking about you to Sam and Mike at practice the other day, saying how awesome you are and that he is psyched you said yes to him asking you to Homecoming. He really does believe you are his good luck charm, you know."

"I really like him too. I hope this dress makes a good impression," Sara said.

"Um, I think it will do a little more than that, if you know what I mean," Kristen said, illustrating her point with obscene hand gestures. They all laughed uncontrollably. Sara felt her face flush from both laughter and embarrassment that she might have that effect on Ethan.

"We have had some pretty hot phone conversations though," Sara said.

"Phone sex, now that is hot," Amy giggled.

"No, not phone sex. He is just so irresistible; his voice makes me weak sometimes," Sara said, feeling a bit self-conscious and maybe like she shouldn't have said anything to them.

"Um, someone has got it bad," Kristen laughed. Sara nudged her shoulder and laughed with them. This had been a great day. Sara needed friends to help boost her confidence.

"Have you and Sam…? You know?" Amy asked Kristen.

"No, we haven't gotten to that point yet in our relationship but anything is possible," Kristen said.

"Mike makes it hard to say no to, but he is always considerate of me. But then again we haven't exactly been dating all that long either and I am not one to sleep around. Not that I wouldn't mind finding out just how big he really is—have you seen the size of his hands?" Amy exclaimed.

Kristen and Sara broke into gut wrenching laughter. They were worse than the guys—Sara would bet on it.

It was a lazy Sunday at Sara's house. Mom sent her to the store to get the ingredients to make her Dad and Brian's favorite 'death by chocolate' cookies. She was going to send Brian a care package and needed a few things from the market. Sara drove to town with her list and parked on the street in front of the market. After wandering the aisles of the market, she paid and grabbed the bags, opening the door and heading out to street where she had parked her car. As she approached, she saw John Waters leaning against it, making himself quite comfortable leaning on her hood.

"Hey, you," John said.

"Are you comfortable?"

"Actually, yes. Doing some shopping?"

"Well, I hate to make you uncomfortable, but would you mind getting off my car?" John slid down and moved away so Sara could open the car door.

"You didn't answer my question."

"Just running some errands for my mom. What about you?" Sara tried to be polite, but every time he spoke she got that uneasy feeling in the pit of her stomach and didn't know why.

"You know, it is pretty coincidental that we keep running into each other." John implied that their chance meetings were intentional.

"I don't think so," Sara said, trying to make him move by swinging the car door wide so she could put the groceries in the car.

"So I hear through the Simpleton grapevine that you joined the cheerleading squad and you and Ethan are a "thing" now," John said , stepping away from the car.

"Yes, you heard correctly. What's it to you?" Sara said.

"Better watch out or you could end up hurt," John said, and walked away.

Sara stood there stunned by what he said. Was he warning her or just acting jealous because she liked Ethan and not him? Sara got into her car and drove home. She spent the rest of the day with her mother baking cookies and trying not to think much about the test results or what John had said. Sunday night Sara was downstairs watching a movie when her phone rang in her bedroom. She tripped going up the stairs and cut her hand on an exposed nail in the banister. The phone kept ringing, but she ignored it to put a bandage on her hand. It bled for a while and after it finally stopped, it looked red and sore. Sara eventually picked up her phone to see who had called. Ethan. She dialed his number to call him back about 7:30 pm.

"Hey," Sara said, happy to hear Ethan's voice.

"Were you busy?" he asked.

"No, how was the game?"

"We killed them, 27-0."

"I thought you needed your good luck charm with you to win."

"You were with me, in my heart." Sara blushed at the sound of his voice saying those words.

"What are you doing right now?"

"Just finishing up some physics homework. What about you?" he said.

"Playing doctor on a self-inflicted wound."

"What happened? Are you okay?"

"Yeah, I just cut my hand. No big deal."

"So, what did you do this weekend?

"I went shopping with the girls for Homecoming; did I mention how excited I am to be going with you?"

"I can't wait to be with you either. Did I mention that I really missed you this weekend? Will I see you tomorrow?"

"Do I have to wait that long?" Sara said, teasing him a bit.

"No, why don't you come over? My parents are working late."

"I will be over in ten minutes," she said. Sara ended the call and butterflies filled her stomach at the thought of being alone with Ethan. She didn't know what had come over her at that moment. She looked at herself in the mirror, brushed her teeth carefully, ran a brush through her hair and dabbed a bit of her favorite perfume behind her ears. She grabbed her favorite sweatshirt and headed downstairs, absent-mindedly leaving her phone on the charger.

Mom had gone to bring dinner and the cookies they had made earlier to Dad at the station so she knew she could just leave a note saying she would be back in a few hours. Sara grabbed some of the cookies for Ethan and drove over to his house faster than she had anticipated. He only lived a few blocks away and she wasn't speeding, but her nervous energy made it feel like she was driving at warp speed. She pulled into the driveway and looked once more at her reflection in the mirror before heading up to the house. Ethan's house was a big stone colonial with a wrap-around porch. The lights were on inside and she could smell a wood fire burning from the chimney. She rang the doorbell once and waited. A moment later, Ethan answered wearing a sleeveless white undershirt and navy blue workout pants.

"Hello beautiful, come in."

"I brought you some of Mom's famous cookies. I helped her make them," She said handing him the bag.

"Tell Mom thanks from me."

Sara stepped inside and smelled a mixture of cinnamon candles and wood smoke. He led her down a long hallway toward a large family room at the back of the house. The room was decorated like a hunting den in dark plaids and leather furniture. A plasma screen television hung above the fireplace. There were candles lit on the mantel. They sat down on the couch and Ethan wasted no time in pulling Sara close to him. He took her bandaged hand into his and touched it gently.

"Does it hurt?" he asked kissing the bandage.

"Not really; it looks worse than it is." Sara was unable able to stop looking at his body. His arms were muscular and strong. His waist so tiny compared to his broad chest and strong legs. She took a deep breath trying to quell those butterflies in her stomach. She had not been this close to him before, nor alone for that matter.

"I really missed you this weekend," he said, gazing deep in to her eyes. His eyes were the color of the ocean, deep blue. You could get lost staring into his eyes. Sometimes at practice Sara would daydream watching him on the field. She had to be careful because the last time she was off in her dreamworld she lost her footing and landed hard on her backside trying to do a back flip.

"I missed you, too," Sara said, softly leaning into him. He smelled clean like soap and freshly laundry.

Ethan reached out his hand and gently touched her face. He leaned in and kissed her softly on the lips.Their first kiss was finally happening,

Sara thought, and it was amazing. Sara's head swirled and her stomach tightened. She closed her eyes and kissed him back not believing what was happening at that moment. Sara had wanted this from the moment she first saw him in the cafeteria. Ethan pulled back and opened his eyes and said, "You have no idea how long I have wanted to do that."

"Me too. I was beginning to think there was something wrong with me or something."

"Now why would you think that?" Ethan asked curiously holding her close.

"Insecurity I guess."

"You have nothing to be insecure about."

"Why did you wait so long to kiss me?"

"I guess I didn't want to rush into things, you know, get to know you better. But every time we were together I just wanted to get closer to you. I wanted to kiss you so badly Friday night, but you just left me standing there on your doorstep. I wasn't sure if I was thinking too much into this," Ethan said.

"And I kept thinking you didn't want to kiss me," Sara said. Ethan softly kissed her again.

"Are you still feeling ill?"

"No, just tired sometimes I guess," Sara said, resting her head on his shoulder. She was elated he had finally kissed her.

"You look a little pale, maybe I can fix that," he said, kissing Sara's neck just below her chin. She was in heaven. Her body tingled all over at the touch of his lips. She had never been this close to a guy before so it was all new to her. His hands roamed her arms and back as he gently rubbed his nose against the hollow of her throat.

"You smell as good as you look," he said, desire in his voice.

"Thanks." Sara didn't know why was still nervous around him. They had been spending almost every free minute together for the last few weeks now. Sara glanced at Ethan's hands, noticing they were scratched and bruised; she assumed from the game. They lay on the couch and continued to kiss softly, getting to know the curves of each other's bodies. Ethan had his hand on Sara's leg as they kissed. He moved his hand slowly to her waist and then up the front of her sweatshirt. Sara took a deep breath and sighed from his warm touch. Just when things started to get interesting the door to the garage opened and Ethan's parents came home.

"Ethan, are you home?" his mother called out.

"Crap, it's my parents!"

They quickly jumped upright into sitting positions, trying not to be conspicuous about what they had been up to. Sara straightened her sweatshirt and tried to smooth out her hair.

"We are in here, Mom," Ethan replied, pulling a pillow in his lap. Sara blushed at this gesture of manly modesty.

"Oh, I saw the car but didn't recognize it. Hi, I am Ethan's mom, Sandra."

"Mom, sorry this is my friend Sara Grady, Chief Grady's daughter," Ethan said.

"It's nice to meet you Mrs. Campbell."

"Nice to finally meet you dear. Ethan, talks about you a lot. I feel like I know you so well. Ethan, did you get some dinner?"

"Yeah, I am fine Mom," Ethan said.

"Well, I'll leave you two to your movie," she said, walking back into the kitchen. Ethan looked annoyed that they had been interrupted. They had been waiting so long to get this close, it was almost a good thing they were interrupted because Sara didn't think she could have stopped herself. He was irresistible in so many ways. Sara glanced at the grandfather clock on the wall. It was getting late and her mom would be back soon. She didn't want her to worry.

"I guess I had better get home," she said, trying not to sound disappointed.

"No, you don't have to leave yet." Ethan seemed insistent.

"I should really be going; Mom will be home soon. See you in the morning?"

"Count on it," Ethan said, and kissed her deeply once more before walking her to the front door. Sara was weak all over from that kiss.

"Good night my sweetness," he said to her as he watched Sara walk to her car.

Sara drove home in a fog. She was so infatuated with him. Ethan was so right in every way and he made her feel good on the inside and out. She loved the way he kissed her. That kiss was so worth waiting for, she thought, Brian was so right. Sara would dream about it. Despite all that, she couldn't stop thinking about how Ethan had introduced her to his mother, as a *friend*. Sara thought to herself *Well, we haven't made any statement to each other that we are a couple. We've been on a few dates and have been spending a lot of time together but neither of us has made any formal statement regarding our relationship.* Sara thought of what John said to her as well. Was Ethan someone she should trust, or was she going to get hurt?

After returning home and getting ready for bed Sara checked her phone and had three missed calls. Amy left a message reminding her to bring her uniform to school tomorrow for school pictures for the yearbook, Brian had called wondering where she was when he tried calling so late on a school night, and the last call was another heavy breather. Sara deleted them all. Who was calling her and leaving those messages? It couldn't possibly be a wrong number, not after the text message. She started freaking out a bit and decided to try some yoga to relax. She turned the phone off and let the meditation exercises take away her tension and anxiety. After several minutes she was calm and decided it was better to not think about this again before going to bed. Instead she lay in bed thinking about her first kiss over and over until she fell asleep.

Chapter 8

Time seemed to be flying by with practice every day. Everyone was making plans for Homecoming weekend. The big game would be followed by the dance and then the after parties. On Wednesday afternoon the phone rang at Sara's home. It was her doctor's office; they had the test results but wanted to schedule an appointment for her to come in and discuss the results in person. *This can't be good*, she thought to herself. Sara's bruises had faded and she was feeling better each day, so really, what could possibly be wrong? She had lost some weight, but with all the physical activity she had been doing lately, it didn't surprise her in the least. Sara decided not to say anything to anyone and to go before school in the morning. She told Ethan that she had an appointment and would see him in biology that afternoon. The appointment was as good as to be expected. Sara's doctor diagnosed her with severe anemia or a lack of iron in the blood. Hence the reason for the bleeding gums, lack of energy, and bruising. She prescribed iron supplements and suggested Sara stick with yoga for some exercise, but not to overdo it. Sara didn't mention the cheerleading because she knew the doctor would tell her to quit the squad. The doctor also said that Sara might have dizzy spells and nausea from time to time and if any of the symptoms got worse to call her right away.

After Sara left the doctor's office she called home and told her mom the diagnosis and was off to school. Mom suggested she come home, but Sara couldn't wait to see Ethan. She tried to look her best despite the paleness of her skin. She was wearing her favorite skinny jeans and boots again and the green sweater she wore on the field trip that Ethan seemed to like so much. Sara wore her hair up and put on some light makeup to give her complexion some color. It was lunchtime when she arrived and the cafeteria was buzzing.

"Where did they find her?" Kristen asked Sam.

"On the old football field out back," Sam replied.

"What's everyone talking about?" Sara said, joining the table in her usual spot.

"They found Calley Bishop out behind the school, she's dead," Mike said.

"Oh my god," Sara gasped, looking at Ethan.

"The school is sending everyone home early so the police can investigate," Amy said.

"When was she found and who found her?" Sara asked.

Mike said he had heard the administrators talking about it in the hall. "A woman was walking her dogs early this morning and she stumbled upon her, same as the other girl, naked and badly beaten."

"There is talk they might cancel the Homecoming game and dance because of this," Kristen said.

"They can't cancel," Amy said, looking at Mike.

"Sara, see what you can find out from your Dad," Sam suggested again, but she didn't bother to protest since she knew she wouldn't be able to get anything out of him. Sara didn't have it in her to bicker with Sam today.

"Hey, why don't we all go to my house for the day?" Mike suggested. "Practice is obviously cancelled and my parents are out of town until next week."

"We will have to clear it with our parents, especially after this happened so close to school," Amy said.

"No problem; besides we are safer in numbers, right?" Ethan said.

Everyone got the okay from their parents to head over to Mike's as long as they stuck together. Sara's mother was a little worried but Sara assured her she was feeling fine. She followed everyone there in her car. Mike's lake house looked even more beautiful during the day. They all piled out of the cars and went up to the house. The entrance way was large enough for the jolly green giant to pass through. The entire back of the house was glass, overlooking the beautiful lake and fall colors of the trees losing their leaves. Mike built a fire and everyone congregated in the living room. There was a pool table and a plasma screen television with all the latest technological gadgets. Mike ordered a movie on pay per view and everyone settled in to watch.

"Do you want the grand tour?" Ethan said to Sara before the movie started.

"Sure," she said as she stood up and followed him.

He took her hand and led the way up the spiral staircase toward the second floor. The house had an open floor plan with cathedral ceilings and exposed beams. It was rustic and cozy. Ethan found the library and led Sara inside.

"This room has the best view of the lake," he said, closing the door as Sara walked toward the windows. Ethan leaned against the door as Sara gazed out the window. She could see his reflection in the glass. Sara's stomach started to flip and her palms were starting to sweat. They were alone again and she so wanted him to kiss her. Ethan came up behind her and put his arms around her waist. He rested his chin on her shoulder and let out a short sigh against her neck.

"I didn't even ask you, how did everything go with your appointment today?" Ethan asked.

"Fine," Sara said, but didn't elaborate.

"Did I tell you how awesome you look today? I really love that sweater on you."

"No," Sara smiled, pulling his arms around her tighter. Ethan kissed her neck and ran his hands over her shoulders. He turned her around with his strong arms and they stood in the middle of the room kissing. His hands found the buttons on her sweater. One by one he undid them.

He lifted her off her feet and laid her on the couch by the window. He stared into Sara's eyes and ran a finger down cheek to her collarbone. She let out a sigh and closed her eyes. Sara's body was screaming from his touch. She wanted him to make the next move. He made her feel incredible and safe, but she was also scared. Scared because this was all new to her and scared because of what was happening around them. All these girls were disappearing and ending up dead. It might be her next, Sara thought. Ethan lifted his shirt over his head and he tossed it on the floor. His abs were so strong and sculpted like a statue. Sara could feel his excitement when he pulled her on his lap kissing her neck. After a moment, she pushed Ethan back with her hand and stopped kissing him.

"Ethan, can I ask you something?"

"Sara you don't have to do anything you don't want to do."

"Wait, what?"

"So what did you want to ask me?" He said, lifting her chin with his finger so Sara was looking straight at him. Confused about what was going on and the fact that they weren't thinking about the same thing at that moment, Sara decided to press on. "The other night when you introduced me to your mom, well, I was just wondering if you really think of me as a friend," Sara stumbled for the right words.

Ethan put his arms around her waist and looked her in the eyes and said, "Of course you are my friend. But I'd like to consider you more than just a friend."

"You mean a friend with benefits?" Sara was insulted.

"No that is not what I mean." He kissed her softly once and said, "Sara, will you be my girlfriend, officially?"

They settled that question with a serious kiss. Sara was so happy and felt so foolish to have thought he had only wanted to be friends. She was just so insecure about herself and couldn't see what interested Ethan so much. Sara couldn't imagine what made her so different from other girls and why he wanted her over the multitude of pretty girls at their school.

There was a knock at the door. "Dude, are you decent?" Mike said.

"Go away," Ethan said to him.

"Seriously E, this is not a panty raid. Okay?" Mike said through the door. Ethan stood up and Sara pulled her sweater closed. Ethan didn't bother to pull his shirt back on before opening the door. He had locked it for safety earlier. "This better be good," he said to Mike as he opened the door a crack.

"E, they arrested Mr. Stone the biology teacher."

Sara jumped up and went toward the door with Ethan. They all went downstairs and watched the breaking news story. The reporter said that an anonymous tip led police to investigate the home of Mr. Stone where they found evidence linking both of the murdered girls to him.

"Oh my god! I can't believe this? Mr. Stone, he seemed like such a nice person," Sara said.

"Who would have thought this could happen in our safe town?" Amy said.

Chief Grady gave a short press conference stating that the investigation uncovered numerous amounts of evidence linking Mr. Stone to the death of both girls and that the District Attorney would be seeking first degree murder charges against him in both cases. Sara called her mom and she told her all about it. Brian had called too to see how things were going. Sara told her she would be home soon and hung up.

"Your dad is the bomb!" Sam said.

"Yeah, I guess he is," Sara said, proud of him. After that, the mood lightened dramatically and the party livened up a bit more. Mike ordered pizzas and everyone carried on like they had just won a football game or something.

Sara pulled Amy into the kitchen and told her about the doctor's appointment. She couldn't stop thinking about it despite everything that was going on.

"I knew something wasn't right with you that day we were shopping. So are you going to keep cheering or is it to dangerous for you?" Amy asked, obviously concerned.

"Look, I don't want anyone else to know, especially Ethan. Things are just too new between us and I don't want to weird him out or anything. I am going to act as if this never happened and just be careful," Sara said.

"Looks like you might want to cover that up a bit," Amy said, pointing to a small hickey on her collarbone.

"Oops, um I wonder how that got there," Sara said, sounding embarrassed.

"Don't worry, Mike is a biter too. Can I ask you a personal question?" Amy said quietly.

"Anything."

"I know the guys are always the ones that should be thinking about being safe in case something happens, but I don't necessarily agree," Amy said.

"I am not following you, what do you mean by safe?"

"Birth control, have you thought about protection at all?"

"I guess I hadn't gotten that far with Ethan yet. I would never be stupid and go unprotected even if I knew Ethan had never been with anyone else before," Sara said.

"Well, I know you don't have a thing to worry about with Ethan. Mike, well, that is another story," Amy said.

"Mike's a slut?" Sara joked.

Amy laughed, "No, but if I had to bet on it, I am probably not going to be his first. Look, I was thinking of going on the pill, and just thought that maybe you would go with me to get it."

"Oh, well, yeah, I will go with you. And maybe you're right. Maybe I should be more responsible about being protected if it ever does happen with Ethan," Sara said.

This was the first time Sara had seen Amy need support rather than give it. It was nice to be needed in that way. "Good, we can go tomorrow," Amy said, hugging her.

Chapter 9

Everyone had the feeling that Simpleton would go back to being the safe town they had always known. Something didn't feel right to Sara though. Perhaps it was the lack of information and the fact that Mr. Stone was caught so quickly despite the lack of evidence found on each girl. Sara knew her father and was confident that he knew how to do his job and do it well. The phone calls had stopped too. Maybe they were connected. What if it had been Mr. Stone stalking Sara? She shuddered at the thought and tried to put that aside and think happy thoughts. Later that night she was still buzzing from what had happened earlier that day and knew she wouldn't be able to fall asleep. She decided to call Ethan and see if he was still awake. "Hello sweetness. What are you doing?" he answered.

"Calling you. I can't believe everything that happened today. What are you up to?"

"I was just laying here in my room thinking about my girlfriend."

"Oh yeah, what are you thinking about?"

"How I wished we weren't interrupted today."

"I know, that keeps happening doesn't it? Cold showers work wonders," Sara said. Ethan laughed.

"I am not sure I can sleep without being next to you tonight," Ethan said.

"Are you alone?" Sara asked him.

"Yes, do you want to come over?" Ethan asked.

"More than you can imagine right now, but I don't know if I can get out of the house without my parents noticing."

"How comfortable are you with lying to them?"

"I wouldn't unless it was for a really good reason. I am not a very good liar."

"Tell them you are going to Amy's to borrow a book or something and you will be back soon."

"I don't know, Ethan."

"Trust me," Ethan pleaded.

Sara contemplated the idea for a moment and said, "Okay, see you in a few minutes." Just to be safe, she called Amy and told her to cover for her.

"Don't do anything I wouldn't do girl," Amy giggled into the phone.

"I owe you big time," Sara said.

She left on her yoga pants and tank top but threw on a zippered sweatshirt so as to not look suspicious. Her parents didn't suspect a thing. Sara drove to Ethan's quickly and parked on the street in case she needed to make a quick exit. She headed to the front door only to see that Ethan was waiting for eagerly for her. He had on shorts and a tight fitting t-shirt. His legs were in great shape and his six pack abs showed through the soft material. "Hi," he said, pulling her out of the cold and into the house. He led Sara upstairs to his room and closed the door. Ethan's room was painted navy blue. Sara sat down on the bed, which was covered with a dark plaid comforter. There was a desk in the corner with a laptop on it and an overstuffed chair next to it. Ethan came toward Sara and kissed her hard, his tongue playing games with hers. He unzipped her sweatshirt and looked down at Sara's body. "How did I ever get so lucky? You know, with you in this outfit, I don't think I can control myself."

"I am having trouble too," Sara said, pulling him to her. Ethan was rock hard with excitement. Sara was eager to touch him but incredibly nervous. She put her hand under his shirt to caress his stomach and he pulled it over his head and threw it across the room. She ran her hand over his firm abs down toward his waist. He kissed her neck and down her shoulder to the strap of her tank top. He pushed the strap down, kissing her shoulder. Sara had goose bumps. Ethan guided Sara's hand down his pants. She was afraid of doing something wrong, of embarrassing herself. She touched him softly at first, having never actually felt a man before. She could feel him tense up and then he let out a soft sigh into her hair. Soon Sara's tank top was off and she was in her bra. She had never gone this far with anyone. She felt like time had stopped. She didn't want to stop but knew it was probably for the best.

"Ethan, wait," Sara said as he was trying to inch her pants off her waist.

"I'm sorry," he said rolling aside. Sara rolled back toward him, not wanting to ruin the moment.

"Look, I really like you and I want to be with you—just not tonight."

"It's okay. I wasn't exactly prepared for this anyway," he said, sitting up.

"Your parents own the pharmacy and you don't have a stash of condoms?" Sara joked.

Ethan laughed, "It's not like I have had loads of girl friends." He put his hands behind his head. "You know I am willing to wait for you whenever you are ready."

"Thank you for understanding," Sara said, pulling her tank top back on. "I should probably go. I think there is a cold shower in my future."

Ethan laughed again and said, "That makes two of us."

Life did go back to normal and thankfully the Homecoming festivities went on as planned. Amy and Sara went to the clinic together after practice one day and while Amy was ready for the pill, Sara decided she wasn't. Things between Amy and Mike were as heated as with Ethan and Sara. Both girls felt strongly that something might happen soon but Sara was nervous about moving too fast. On the way home from the clinic, Sara told Amy about what John Waters had said to that day outside the market.

"Don't listen to anything he said to you," Amy said angrily.

"Why?"

"There is history between John and Ethan and John is just jealous of him."

"Wait, explain yourself," Sara said.

"Did you know that Calley Bishop and Mike used to date?" Amy said.

"No. When?" Sara asked, curious that Amy hadn't mentioned it before now.

"Back when we were freshman, Mike and Calley dated for a few months, nothing serious. She dated John Waters after that."

"Really? So you don't think I have anything to worry about with Ethan?"

"Ethan is a safe as they come. We are so lucky to have the most loyal, trusting boyfriends," Amy said. It was the first time Sara heard that phrase out loud about Ethan.

Then reality sank in. "I guess it's true, Ethan is my boyfriend."

"You know he is crazy about you, right?"

"You think so? I mean, how do you know for sure?"

"Mike told me that Ethan was out with him the other day after practice and he told him he is falling for you hard. He said that he was really looking forward to this weekend and being alone with you," Amy said.

"Okay if I wasn't nervous before, I am seriously nervous now! What if I say the wrong things or do something to make myself look like a dork?"

"Hey, calm down. Ethan cares about you no matter what. If the time is right, things will happen. If not he will wait for you and you don't have to worry about him pressuring you," Amy said reassuringly.

"Thanks, Amy. If it wasn't for you, I wouldn't have met Ethan."

"What are friends for?"

As expected, Simpleton High won the Homecoming football game and had an undefeated record that school year. Ethan was voted MVP of the game and carried on the shoulders of the team. Despite being the center of attention, all Ethan wanted to do was be with Sara. She ran up to him in her cheerleading uniform and hugged him tightly. He was sweaty and tired, but kissed Sara in front of the crowd like in a dream and swept her off her feet. Sara was so proud of him and the team.

Everyone was excited about the dance. Amy and Kristen decided to get ready at Sara's house and the guys were going to pick them up there. After an hour of primping and styling their hair the girls were almost ready. The doorbell rang, startling them—the guys were there. Sara was the last to slip into her dress. All traces of the bruises were gone and she had gained some color back in her face. She looked at herself in the mirror and couldn't believe that was her staring back. Amy had pulled Sara's hair up into a chignon leaving soft tendrils of blond hair falling around her face. She gave Sara smokey eyes with soft pale lips. Sara chose silver stilettos and long silver earrings to complement the unbelievably sexy dress. From the front it looked as though she was wearing a sleeveless cocktail dress that showed off the muscle tone in her arms and collar bones from all the recent workouts from cheerleading, but from the back it was a different story altogether. Sara took a deep breath. Her dad was going to have a heart attack when he saw her in this dress; his little girl all grown up. Amy and Kristen were gorgeous as usual, but they both agreed that Sara was hands down the best looking tonight. They made their way carefully downstairs—trying not to trip on the stairs—to where Ethan, Mike and Sam were waiting for them.

The guys' mouths gaped open at first glance. Each went to their date and Sara's mom made them all pose for way too many pictures. Ethan kissed Sara on the cheek in front of her parents politely and pressed his hand into the small of her exposed back. He hadn't seen her from behind yet. He leaned back and glanced at the dress and then gripped Sara's waist tightly. "Wow," he whispered in her ear excitedly.

"You kids have a great time tonight and be safe," Sara's mom said.

"I will see you tomorrow," Sara said to her as they walked out the door. Her parents were not high on her staying out all night, but she was a senior and things had gone back to normal again in Simpleton so they both agreed to let her stay out. They all left for the dance in separate cars planning to meet up when they got there. Ethan opened the door for her as Sara gingerly stepped down into his Mustang. He closed the door and raced to his side. Sara's dress was form-fitting and when she sat it hitched up her thigh a bit. Ethan kept one hand on the wheel and the other on Sara for the entire drive.

"Holy hotness—that dress. I mean, Sara, you look incredible," he said with an enormous smile. Ethan looked gorgeous too. He was wearing a charcoal-gray suit with a navy shirt and tie.

"You look pretty hot yourself," Sara said, playing with his tie.

"Thanks, but that dress is screaming at me to take it off you."

"Be good now. Who knows what the night will bring?"

She felt like the most special person in the world that night. Ethan kept her close and kissed her neck every chance he got. Sara was on top of the world. They all danced and celebrated the best night of their lives. It was nearing the end of the dance and they were about to announce the Homecoming King and Queen. Amy, Kristen, and Sara huddled together, hoping it would be one of them. They announced the King first—and to no one's surprise they called Ethan's name. Sara was so proud of him and even more psyched that he had chosen her to spend the evening with. They crowned him and handed him the envelope for Queen. A drum roll hushed the crowd and Ethan announced Amy's name. They were all jumping up and down excited as hell for her. Sara was a little disappointed, but still really happy for her. It would have been truly a dream come true if both Ethan and Sara were crowned together. The dance ended with her favorite song, *In Your Eyes*, and they all headed out to Mike's house for the after party. Mike's parents' lake house had become the hangout for the high school crowd. The place was decorated to the hilt. Lights twinkled everywhere, making it seem like every inch of the place was dripping with icicles. The weather had turned colder and it felt like it would snow.

After everyone arrived and the party was in full swing Ethan took Sara's hand, "I have a surprise for you." He led her up the staircase back to the library. Apparently the guys had been busy while they were preparing for the dance. Ethan had filled the library with candles and dusted the floor with red rose petals. He remembered what Sara had said about her perfect date. It was the most romantic thing she had ever seen. The moonlight shone off the lake through the windows and the candles gave off a soft glow illuminating the room.

"Ethan, this is like a dream, it's amazing," Sara whispered.

"No. You are amazing. I can't believe how incredible you look tonight. I always knew you were gorgeous but tonight I felt like you were mine and only mine." Sara kissed him softly. She kicked off her heels and let her hair down. He kissed her neck and ran his fingers down her back.

"I am glad you liked it, I picked it out especially for you."

Ethan suddenly got serious and said, "Sara, I have never been this crazy about anyone before. I am really falling for you hard. I haven't been with that many girls and I have been hurt badly before."

"Ethan, no one has ever made me feel as special and wanted as you do. I feel so safe with you. You make me feel beautiful on the inside and out," Sara said. She loosened his tie and began to unbutton his shirt. She slid his shirt off his shoulders and kissed his chest. He dipped his head and traced his fingers down her spine. Nervously, Sara slipped out of her dress revealing her black lace panties and backless bra. Ethan's eyes widened with excitement and he pulled her closer to him. "I still can't believe you are mine. But seeing you dressed like that makes it really hard to control myself," he said.

"I trust you, Ethan," Sara said shyly.

"Are you sure?" he asked eagerly. Sara nodded at him. She wanted to be with him at that moment even though she wasn't sure what to do. Ethan kissed her hard, picking her up off the floor and placing her on top of the petal-covered blanket. He kissed her shoulders, arms, and made his way down to her stomach. He kissed every inch of Sara's skin making her writhe with desire for him. Sara could feel his muscles tense. She nervously played with the button of his pants.

"Ethan, I've never done this before. I mean…." Sara tried to say the right thing without sounding totally stupid.

He stopped kissing her, looked her in the eyes, and said, "Neither have I." In that instant she knew tonight would be the most perfect night of their lives. They were about to share something so special that would stay with them forever no matter what happened. Sara was freaking out. Her breathing was erratic; she tried desperately to slow it down. She wanted to be with him but was so nervous. What was she getting herself into here? Was she making the right decision?

"Do you have something?" Sara whispered nervously in his ear.

"Uh huh."

"Came prepared didn't you?" Sara asked him, joking to ease some of her nervousness.

"I wasn't sure what would happen. Honestly, I was hoping this would happen," he said, looking into her eyes. Sara undid his belt buckle and he slid his pants off. His boxers couldn't hide his excitement. He rolled her over and they kissed deeply. She was so nervous. He seemed so in control of everything and not the least bit nervous. Sara pulled the blanket over them and they made love in the moonlight. Ethan touched her in ways she had never imagined. He was so gentle. He made Sara feel beautiful inside and out. He felt incredible. His body was so strong and well equipped. When it was over they lay in each others' arms blissfully.

"Sara," Ethan said rolling over and reaching for something under the couch. "Can I ask you something?"

"Anything," Sara replied .

"Would you wear my ring?" He opened his hand revealed a small box.

"Your class ring?"

"I know we have only been dating a short time, but I know how I feel about you. If you wear my ring it means that you are mine and no other guy can have you," he said with the brightest smile Sara had ever seen. Sara didn't know what to say. Everything was happening so fast. They had gone from waiting so long to kiss to sleeping with each other. Was she sure this is what she wanted? Without thinking another moment about it Sara blurted out, "Yes." Ethan opened the box and slipped out a silver ring with a square sapphire in the center. It was huge but he had thought of that and slipped it on a silver rope chain and put it around her neck.

"Ethan, what if we hadn't done it tonight—would you still want me to wear your ring?"

"Sara, being together tonight only makes it that much more real the way I feel about you. But to answer your question, yes, I would have wanted you to wear my ring regardless of what did or didn't happen here tonight," Ethan said. He put his arms around her and held her close, stroking her hair. They fell asleep in each other's arms happy and falling in love with each other.

Chapter 10

The next morning Sara woke very early. It was still dark outside; the sun was just starting to come up over the horizon. Sara pulled on Ethan's shirt over her dress, trying not to wake him, and ventured out to find a bathroom. There were a few people left from the night before sleeping randomly through the house. Sara almost tripped over several of them making her way to the kitchen. Amy and Kristen were already awake and sipping hot chocolate in the breakfast nook covered in a blanket.

"Hey, morning," Sara said to them with a sleepy grin.

"Where did you disappear to last night?" Amy said.

"The library," Sara said with a grin, showing them the ring around her neck.

"You aren't the only one that got a lovely memento last night," Amy said, tilting her head to reveal an enormous love bite on her neck that she had tried her best to cover with her hair. Kristen looked tired but happy as well.

"What a night," Sara said, sitting down next to them after grabbing a steaming cup of hot chocolate for herself.

"I think this was the best night of our lives," Kristen said. They giggled together and sat sipping hot chocolates.

"Those guys went out of their way to make last night special. I am really going to miss this next year when we are away in college," Kristin said with tears in her eyes.

"Oh now, don't get all emotional on us," Amy said to her.

"I wonder what is going to happen with Mr. Stone," Sara said.

"I still can't believe that he was the one that did those horrible things," Amy said.

"I know, he was my biology teacher. He never made me uncomfortable or anything like that. Hey, let me ask you both something?"

"Shoot," Kristin said, sipping her drink.

"Have either of you been getting hang-ups or prank calls lately?"

"No," Amy said.

"I haven't gotten any, why?" Kristen added.

"Well, I have been getting these phone calls for weeks now and then when Mr. Stone was arrested, they stopped."

"Did you mention it to your dad?" Amy asked.

"No, I figured it was some prank or something but then when we went shopping that day for dresses, I got a picture message and it said 'I am watching you'. The photo was the three of us in the store that day," Sara said, thinking back.

"Wait, why didn't you tell us then?" Kristin said, sounding worried.

"I don't know, I didn't want to worry anyone," Sara said. It got quiet for a minute.

"You said that the calls stopped after Mr. Stone was arrested?" Amy asked.

"Yes, I haven't had one since. Look I am sorry I didn't say anything before" Sara said, feeling guilty that she hadn't told them before now. "Did you guys know those girls well, Kim and Calley?"

"No, I mean we all hung around together when we were younger. Mike dated Calley Bishop when we were freshman and Ethan dated Kim Randall," Kristen said.

"What…?" Sara said. Her face went pale with shock.

"Didn't he tell you? Remember when I told you he dated someone and it ended badly a few years ago? I just assumed he told you," Amy said, surprised.

"He never said anything. I mean, I asked him if he knew her and he just said that she was a partier and that he knew her when he was younger," Sara responded in shock. Thoughts were swirling in her head. *Why wouldn't he tell me he knew her? Was he not telling me the whole story?* Sara suddenly felt nauseous. The room began to spin.

"Sara, are you felling all right?" Amy asked her. Sara tried to close her eyes to stop the room from spinning.

"Um, no I think I need to lie down," Sara said, trying to get up and leave the room. Suddenly the room grew dark and she passed out.

"Holy crap, Sara, Sara!" Amy jumped up and put the blanket under her head. "Quick, get the guys," Amy shouted to Kristen.

"Ethan, Mike, Sam! Come quick, it's Sara!" Kristen yelled up the stairs. The guys flew out of their rooms and down the stairs half dressed. Sara lay on the floor still unconscious. Ethan, still in his boxers, dove to his knees cradling her head on the floor. "What happened?" he yelled at Amy.

"I don't know, we were talking about the murders and how you and Mike knew them and the next thing we know Sara's on the floor passed out," Amy responded.

"Should we call for help?" Sam asked, trying to stay calm.

"She is breathing, her pulse is normal. I think she just passed out," Ethan said. "Sara, wake up. Sara, are you all right?" Ethan sounded worried.

Amy didn't say anything to anyone but knew what was really going on.

Sara could hear him but it sounded like he was talking through a fog. With her eyes closed she said, "Yes."

"Holy crap, what happened to you?" Mike asked.

Sara slowly opened her eyes and saw everyone standing over her in the kitchen. She was embarrassed and didn't want to talk about what was going on with her.

"I am fine; I didn't eat last night. I just fainted, sorry to worry you all like that," Sara said, blushing and letting the color come back into her face.

"Well, *that* was a wake up call. Let's get this place cleaned up," Mike said, surveying the damage from the party.

"I think you had better just sit here for a while. Do you want some juice or something?" Ethan said to her, with a concerned look that made Sara feel that fainting was almost worth the trouble.

"No, I'm fine. Really," Sara said, trying to smile. She felt horrible inside. Why hadn't he told her the truth? Was he embarrassed by his past? Or was it something else? Ethan and the guys went to clean up the house and get dressed. Amy sat with Sara in the kitchen.

"I was so worried about you. You have to say something to Ethan," Amy said to her with concern in her voice.

"No. I mean not yet. I need to know why he didn't tell me about Kim. Why did he lie to me?"

Later that morning, everyone left the lake house and Ethan drove Sara home. She was quiet most of the drive. When he pulled into her driveway he cut the engine and turned to face her. "Are you sure you are feeling okay? I didn't hurt you last night, did I?" he asked, putting his hand on hers.

"I am fine, really," Sara said, trying to find the right words to ask him what was going on.

"You've been so quiet, did I do something wrong?"

"Ethan, I have to ask you something. Why didn't you tell me you dated Kim Randall when I asked if you knew her?"

"Who told you?" He said, looking straight ahead now and gripping the steering wheel.

"Amy, but what does that have to do with it? Did you sleep with her?"

"I didn't want to tell you because it was a long time ago. No, we didn't sleep together. Kim broke up with me, treated me like dirt and cheated on me with John Waters. It took me a long time to get over that and honestly, you are the first person I have been serious about since then." He spoke with sincerity, still looking out the windshield.

It wasn't the response Sara was expecting. She felt sorry for Ethan. How could she think such horrible thoughts about him? Sara leaned over, pulling his face toward hers, and kissed him softly.

"I am sorry I brought up bad memories, especially after last night," Sara said, touching the ring on her neck.

"I'll call you later," he said as she got out of the car and watched him drive down the street. Sara was feeling horrible both emotionally and physically. Had she just screwed up everything with the first serious relationship she had ever had?

After a long shower and a nap she called Brian. "So, how was the big night? Did you get crowned Homecoming Queen or what?" Brian said.

"No, but Ethan was crowned King. How 'bout them apples?" Sara said smugly.

"Well, so does that make you Queen by association? How are you feeling?" Sara told him about the fainting spell and asked him not to say anything to Mom and Dad.

"Sara, you have to be careful. Not enough iron can lead to all sorts of bad things including liver failure or worse—you could bleed out if you got cut badly."

"Well, I will try to be careful. How are things at school?"

"Pretty grueling actually. Pre-med is kicking my ass this semester. I did meet someone though. Her name is Samantha, she is a fox and also pre-med," Brian said with a laugh.

"Good for you. Do we get to meet her this holiday season?"

"Maybe. Heard the news about Dad. How are things in town?

"Getting back to normal I guess."

"I have to run to meet Samantha, but you hang in there and try not to overdo it kiddo."

"Call you soon."

"Bye."

Later that night as Sara was prepping for school her cell phone rang.

"Hey," she said, answering after she saw Ethan's number.

"What are you doing?"

"Just getting stuff ready for tomorrow. Why?"

"We need to talk," he said. Sara got a sinking feeling in the pit of her stomach. Those words had always meant something horrible when she had heard them before. Sara dropped to the floor and leaned against the bed for support. "Look, I am sorry I didn't say anything to you about Kim. I didn't want you to get the wrong idea or anything."

"I understand, but we don't have to talk about it again. I promise," Sara said feeling terrible for the things she was thinking earlier. "Ethan, about last night, I just wanted you to know how special it was for me. You make me feel better than anyone has ever made me feel about myself,"

"You have no idea how much you mean to me, do you?"

"Ethan, I have never been this serious with anyone before. Things just started moving so fast between us, I guess I am just a little scared where all this is headed."

"What are you saying? You are scared of me; why?" Ethan sounded uneasy.

"I just have never felt these incredible emotions before and I don't really know what to say is all. You are the first for me in more ways than one."

"I told you Sara, you were the first person that I have ever been with. I may have dated more than you but that doesn't mean I have been in intimate relationships with them. Look, we don't have to rush into things. When the time is right for us we will know. I promise. For now let's just keep things easy and uncomplicated.".

"So do you still want me to wear your ring?" Sara asked, feeling sick to her stomach with worry that she had messed things up.

"I hope you never take it off." Ethan said, to her relief.

"Not even when I shower?" Sara tried a joke to lighten the mood.

"Especially not then; I want to be as close to your body as possible at all times. How about I pick you up tomorrow morning?"

"Deal. I had better get some sleep. See you tomorrow," Sara said, hanging up.

Well, that was a conversation I don't want to relive in the future, she thought to herself as she sat on the floor. It was amazing how fast her life could go from top of the world to crap, and back again, in a matter of hours. Sara wondered what was in store for the future.

Chapter 11

November had arrived and the football season was nearing its end. The weather had turned bitter cold overnight. Snow was in the forecast just about daily. The team was on to the state championships and Ethan was nominated for all-state most valuable player. College scouts were at every game, making the guys want to play harder and win that much more. Practices became longer each day and Ethan and Sara spent less and less time together. They just had so much on their plates with school, practice, and the state championships around the corner they were stretched thin. One day at school Sara was on her way to lunch alone when she bumped into John Waters.

"Well, look at what we have here," John said.

"Hi," Sara said, and tried to move past him into the cafeteria.

"All alone today?"

"No," Sara responded sharply, again trying to pass him.

"So, why don't you dump that boyfriend of yours and let me take you on a real date?"

"Excuse me?" Sara said, stopping dead in her tracks.

"You heard me. I can show you how a real woman should be treated," John was blocking her way into the cafeteria. She tried to push past him but he wouldn't budge. Sara was thoroughly annoyed by him at this point and she grabbed his arm to move it aside when Ethan and Amy came around the corner.

"Let her past, Waters," Ethan growled at John.

"I was just telling your girl here that I can treat her better than you can. Just look at your old girlfriend. Oh wait, she's dead isn't she?" John said as he turned and walked away.

Ethan hit his breaking point and lunged at John shoving him against the lockers. "Ethan don't!" Sara yelled, trying to pull them apart. She was not sure who swung first, but all she remembered was a hand shoving her hard and knocking her head first into the lockers. Blood filled her mouth and ran down the right corner of her lower lip. Sara wiped at her mouth with her hand and blood covered it.

"Oh my god! Sara, are you all right?" Amy said, helping her to her feet and whisking them to the bathroom before any of the teachers saw what happened.

"This isn't over!" John said to Ethan, giving him a stone cold look as he shoved open the doors and exited the building.

Ethan waited patiently outside the bathroom. Meanwhile, Amy was trying to help stop the bleeding and cover the red mark on Sara's cheek from where she made contact with the metal lockers.

"Sara, it won't stop," Amy said, sounding worried. Sara held the tissue against her lip with some pressure. After a few minutes it did stop, but she was light headed. Sara thought she might have a slight concussion, but didn't want to say anything. "What happened out there?" Amy asked.

"John was being a real jerk, wouldn't let me past him, and that is when you guys showed up."

"I have never seen Ethan react that way in all the years I have known him. John really set him off," Amy said.

"I know things have been pretty stressed these past few weeks and all, but do you think it's something else?" Sara asked her.

"Like what?"

"I don't know—that is what is worrying me."

"Come on, I am sure Ethan is outside worried to death about you,"

Amy said, leading her toward the bathroom door. Sara gave herself a last glance in the mirror. The red spot was fading on her cheek but the lip was going to leave a bruise. She was going to have to come up with a story for her parents to cover this one for sure. She stepped out into the hall just outside the cafeteria where Ethan was leaning against the wall waiting for them.

"Sara, are you okay?" Ethan put his arms around her. He held her tightly.

"Yeah," Sara looked down at the floor.

"I am going inside, can I get you anything?" Amy asked.

"Something with ice please."

"No, nothing for me," Ethan said. He let go of her and said, "Sara, I am so sorry. I don't know what happened. John just totally set me off. I feel horrible that you got hurt. I swear I will never do anything like that again."

"What's going on with you Ethan? You have never been so short fused," Sara asked, looking him directly in the face.

"Nothing! I mean I am just stressed you know. I never imagined how much the team was counting on me to make the right decisions. My parents are really hounding me to make a decision about college too. I haven't been able to spend any time with you either."

"Oh," was all she could manage.

"Are you mad at me?" Ethan asked.

"No and listen, don't worry about spending time with me. We will see each other when we can, right? Plus you can always call me anytime. Besides, I am not going anywhere and you can make it up to me after the season is over and we are so bored we won't know what to do," Sara said, trying to sound confident but with that sinking feeling in her stomach again.

Ethan hugged her and kissed her softly trying not to hurt the swollen lip. That was the last time she was going to let John Waters interfere in her relationship with Ethan. Fortunately by the time she got home that afternoon her lip went back to normal.

Things had gone back to normal in Simpleton or at least so it seemed. A few weeks had passed since Mr. Stone had been arrested. The investigation seemed to be over for the most part and then, when least expected, it happened again—another girl disappeared.

The phone rang late one night and Sara's dad answered, "Chief Grady here. I understand. I will be there as soon as I can."

"Bill, what happened?" Sara's mom said to him quietly.

"Another girl has gone missing; we are setting up search parties."

Sara closed her bedroom door and picked up her cell phone to call Amy. Sleepily Amy answered, "Sara, what's up?"

"Someone else went missing," Sara said, fear in her voice.

"Who? When?" Amy was suddenly wide awake.

"I am not sure yet, but it will make the news for sure soon. Maybe Mr. Stone wasn't the one doing this. Maybe he was set up? Maybe the real killer is still out there," she said, trying to make sense of it all.

"Should we call the guys, tell them what's going on?" Amy suggested.

"I am sure they will all find out by morning. Let's not do anything just yet. Please don't go out alone from now on, okay? Tell Kristin I said the same thing."

"Who do you think is doing this?" Amy asked.

"I don't know. Amy, what happened really between Kim and Ethan?" Sara asked. She hadn't brought it up again to Ethan but it was still on her mind.

"Oh girl, Kim really messed Ethan up badly. They were dating really serious when we were freshman. Ethan had given her a promise ring and everything. They spent all their time together, like they were inseparable. We used to joke that they would end up the couple most likely to get married after graduation. Then Ethan tried out for the team and beat out John Waters for the quarterback spot. John was really angry and decided to quit the team. Then one day, out of the blue, Kim just broke up with him. She told him that she was dating John and didn't want to be with him anymore. Ethan was crushed and wouldn't date anyone for the longest time, no one serious anyway. Kim and John only lasted a short time though. John and Ethan couldn't stand being around one another so John just pulled away from everyone after that. Several months later John dumped Kim and started dating Calley which then pissed off Mike. You see where the story is going?"

"That explains why Ethan was so pissed that day in biology that first week I met you guys and the scene the other day at school," Sara said, remembering why he didn't talk to her at first. Sara had been talking with John, being friendly toward him. But after what John said to her she couldn't imagine how Ethan didn't tear his head off.

"Oh Sara, don't worry. Ethan knows you are not like Kim. He obviously cares for you a great deal, otherwise he wouldn't be putting his heart out there again. I mean you are wearing his ring, right?"

"Yes, I guess you are right. We talked things out and I think things are fine now between us, but…" Sara trailed off. "Can you keep a secret?"

"Sara, I consider you my best friend. You and Kristin are my rocks. I would keep anything secret that you asked me," Amy replied.

"Ethan and I…we sort of did it Homecoming night at Mike's house," Sara said, trying not to be embarrassed about her amazing experience with Ethan.

"Oh my gosh! I knew it that morning. You had that look on your face," Amy gushed. " Ethan wasn't the only guy to get lucky that night," Amy said, giggling.

"Wait, you and Mike did it too?" Sara asked her, kind of shocked.

"And Kristin and Sam too. Mike told me he loved me and that he had been waiting for me to make the first move for a long time. Were you nervous?" Amy said.

"Are you kidding me, I am lucky I didn't faint several times before that next morning. I am so happy for you. Wait, you said Kristin and Sam?" Sara said, shocked by what she thought was a huge secret.

"I guess it was a magical night for all of us," Amy said.

"I never would have imagined a night being more perfect in my life. Amy, I think I am falling in love with Ethan," Sara said.

"I don't see how he isn't in love with you already. Have you told him that?" Amy said.

"No, please don't say anything to him. I know he cares a lot for me, but I am not sure he is in love with me and we both agreed to slow things down a bit," Sara said.

"Wait, you are slowing things down. Why?" Amy asked.

"Our hormones were just raging when we are together and honestly I am not sure I am ready for things to be so serious so soon. We are not breaking up or anything, I am new at this whole relationship thing and telling him I love him might make things complicated again," Sara said.

"Oh yeah, you are a virgin in this relationship. Not!" Amy joked with her.

"Shut up. See you tomorrow," Sara said hanging up the phone. The smile left her face as reality set in and Sara realized that this wasn't a time to be thinking about herself. Another girl had gone missing or possibly worse. Was she in danger?

The next day the news of the missing girl—Amanda Bradford, this one from the next town over and another school—spread like wildfire. Apparently she was last seen with a bunch of people out Friday night at a party after a football game. She never came home.

Amy and Sara made their way into the cafeteria that next day and found Kristin sitting alone at their usual spot looking distraught. "Kristin, what's wrong?" Sara said sitting next to her and putting a hand on her shoulder.

"You know the girl that went missing, Amanda?" Kristin said.

"Yeah, what about her?" Amy said.

"I just found out that she and Sam used to date a few years ago," Kristin said. A sick feeling spread through Sara's body as she fought back a wave of nausea. The girls looked at one another all thinking the same thing. Each of the girls that had gone missing had dated their boyfriends in the past.

"Do you think it could be connected to them? I mean, where was Sam on Friday night?" Sara asked.

"He was with Mike and Ethan, right?" Amy said.

"Yes, but do you think we are in danger? I mean you don't think the guys had anything to do with this do you?" Kristin said.

"Don't be ridiculous, that is absurd. Those guys are the sweetest, most caring and harmless people in the world and they would never hurt anyone," Amy responded sharply. They sat there not saying anything until the crowd came to join them at the table. No one mentioned it again that day.

Chapter 12

Ethan and Sara had been trying to spend more time together since their talk. His parents had gotten used to seeing Sara around on the weekends and so did Sara's mom during school nights. Sara's dad was always at work lately so he didn't seem bothered by Ethan's constant presence in her home. Sara's mom actually enjoyed having someone else to cook for. She has been trying out new recipes on them hoping to concoct the perfect one for a contest in the spring.

"Your dad said they might release Mr. Stone if the evidence shows that this new girl is connected to the original case," Mom said.

"What? They don't think he did it anymore?" Sara was concerned.

"If your dad can't prove otherwise or find Amanda soon he will go free until the trial," Mom said. Sara looked at Ethan with worry.

"I am going to bring Dad some supper. Ethan, will you stay with Sara until I get back?" Mom asked.

"Sure Mrs. Grady, no problem." Ethan grinned at Sara with his gorgeous smile. She could tell what was on his mind and avoided direct eye contact while her mom was still in the room.

Sara's mom left shortly after that for the station and Ethan and Sara went up to her room to hang out. This was the first time they had been alone in her room together.

"So, what do you want to do?" Sara asked him shyly.

"Hmmm…Let's get comfy and watch a movie," Ethan said. Sara pulled the blankets off the bed and they cuddled in her oversized chair together. There wasn't much on that night.

"So, I was wondering, do you ski?" Ethan asked.

"Um yeah, I am from upstate New York, remember, the snow belt. Why?" Sara asked.

"Well, the guys were talking about taking a ski weekend to Mike's parents' chalet in the mountains over Christmas break and I thought you might want to come with us. Actually, we were all hoping you girls would want to come."

"I think that sounds awesome, but I have to warn you I will ski circles around you," Sara said, tracing a tiny circle on his chest with her finger. Ethan kissed Sara softly.

She kissed him back with a little more energy than the last kiss. Something inside her came to life at that point and she knew she wanted to be with him right then. "This chair is a little tight for the two of us," Sara said, getting up and lying on her bed. Ethan followed her and kissed her again. They were making out for a while, going slowly to avoid getting carried away. Between kisses Sara said, "Ethan, I…" But he kissed her before she could tell him that she was falling in love with him. Just as she was about to try again her cell phone rang and interrupted them. "Hold that thought," Sara said to him and answered the phone. Nothing but heavy breathing again.

"Okay whoever this is, stop calling me," Sara said and hung up, turning the cell phone off.

"What the hell what that all about?" Ethan asked.

"Nothing, just some idiot's idea of a prank. I have been getting these heavy breathing calls for a while now; I have no idea from whom," Sara said feeling angry.

"Wait, why didn't you say anything before now?" Ethan said sounding annoyed.

"Because they stopped for a while and then Amanda went missing and they started up again."

"Have you told anyone else—like maybe your dad?" Ethan asked.

"Well, no, I haven't said anything to him, but I have said something to Amy and Kristin. I wanted to see if it was just me or if they were getting calls, too."

"Were they?"

"No." Sara didn't know what else to say at that point. Ethan got up from the bed and crossed the room.

Just then Sara's mother returned and Ethan said, "I should be going now. It is getting late."

"Don't be mad at me for not telling you."

"I am not mad, just worried. I don't think this is a joke, Sara."

A week went by and still there was no sign of Amanda. Mid-terms were coming up soon. Sara was at Ethan's house one night studying for their biology exam. It was getting pretty late and they had lost track of time. Sara stretched her arms and lay back on the floor. Ethan stopped reviewing and rolled on top of her. He kissed her and said, "Do you know how much I want you right now?"

"Even after hours of studying and in this old sweatshirt?" Sara tugged at her favorite Harvard sweatshirt.

"I am thinking that we might have to take this off of you, so I can be absolutely sure," he said with a grin. He pulled her sweatshirt over her head in one fluid motion and Sara lay back on the floor in only her sports bra. She rolled over onto her stomach, playing hard to get.

"Sara, what happened to your back?" Ethan said, putting his hands on her.

"It's nothing." Sara grabbed her sweatshirt and pulled it over her head quickly to hide the bruises.

"What's going on? How did you get those bruises?"

Sara looked down and tried not to make him worry. "Ethan, I haven't been totally honest with you. I have a condition called severe anemia. My blood lacks iron so I bruise really easily and I get tired a lot too. I found out a while ago when I was sick with the flu. I didn't want to say anything because we were just getting to know each other and I didn't want you to be freaked out or, worse, feel sorry for me. That is why I fainted that morning after Homecoming."

"Sara, why would you think that? Sweetness, I care about you, all of you," he said, kissing her forehead.

"I care about you too, maybe more than you can comprehend," Sara said. She wanted to tell him that she was falling in love with him, but couldn't. She was afraid he might not feel the same. There was a big difference between love and a strong crush. It was late and she knew that she had better get going or they would both fail their exams the next day. Ethan walked Sara to her car. It was freezing out and the weathermen predicted snow for the weekend. Sara started the car to let it warm up.

"I will see you tomorrow, okay?" Ethan said, hugging her tightly.

"Not if I see you first!"

What happened next was like a dream—only Sara was awake. Ethan nuzzled her ear with his cold nose and said, "I love you." She pulled back to look at his face. He was smiling his gorgeous smile and opened the door for her. Sara got into the car in a daze, unable to speak. Ethan had just told her he loved her and she couldn't respond. Ethan waved and headed back toward his house. Sara drove the few blocks home replaying the moment over and over in her head. Up ahead at the stop sign there was a car with its flashers on. Sara slowed up to see if she knew the person. It was John Waters. Sara contemplated not stopping, thinking of the way he treated Ethan and Mike, but decided to stop anyway. She rolled down her window and offered her help.

"Hey, what happened?" Sara called out to him.

"Not sure, it just stopped and now it won't start," he said, looking under the hood.

"I can call a tow truck for you."

"That would be great," John said approaching her car. Sara leaned across the seat to grab her phone out of her bag and the next thing she knew John had struck her on the head with a tire iron. Sara slumped down in her seat and blacked out. John pulled her out of the car and threw her into the back seat of his car leaving Sara's car at the stop sign still running.

Chapter 13

The phone rang at Ethan's house later that night. "Hello Mr. Campbell, this is Chief Grady. Is Sara still there?"

"No, I think she left hours ago. Did she not make it home?" Mr. Campbell asked, concerned.

"No she didn't and she isn't answering her cell phone either."

"Hold on, I'll get Ethan," Mr. Campbell said. "Ethan, its Chief Grady on the phone. What time did Sara leave tonight?" Mr. Campbell said as he turned on the light.

Ethan jumped out of bed and said, "Why? Is she all right?"

"She never made it home," Mr. Campbell said.

Ethan thought for a minute, "It was around 10:30 when she left."

Mr. Campbell relayed the information to Sara's dad and hung up the phone. Ethan was throwing on his clothes and rummaging around for his keys. "Son, where are you going?" Mr. Campbell said.

"I have to go look for her. She was only a few minutes from home. Something must have happened to her." Ethan grabbed his keys and flew out the door to his car. He sped out of the driveway and traced back the route he thought Sara would have taken home.

He saw the Mustang abandoned at the stop sign and dialed Sara's dad.

"Chief Grady, it's Ethan. I just found Sara's car."

"I'm on my way, don't touch a thing," Chief Grady said, running out of the house. He came rushing to the scene with his lights flashing and siren on. He saw the car, the blood on the front seat, and his heart sank. "My god, what the hell happened to her?"

"We have to find her," Ethan said, hysterical.

"You are damn right," he said, calling in the crime scene unit. The dark street was soon filled with flashing lights from patrol cars and the crime scene unit taking pictures. There weren't any houses nearby so there were no witnesses. They dusted the car for prints and took samples of blood for testing. Sara's cell phone was on the front seat where she had left it.

The sky was growing light by the time things had wrapped up. The car was driven home by one of the patrolmen. Ethan was sent home to wait until he heard from Sara's dad. Ethan couldn't sleep. Thoughts wandered in his mind keeping him awake.

The next morning Ethan still hadn't heard anything from Sara's dad. He was going crazy not knowing what happened to her. Ethan called Mike. "Dude, we just heard what happened. How are you holding up, man?" Mike said.

"Going out of my damn mind! We have to find her before that sick bastard does anything to hurt her," Ethan said.

"I'll get Sam and the girls together and we will meet you at the school. There is some connection to us and if we figure it out maybe we will find Sara," Mike said, trying to sound hopeful.

A little while later they all met up at the high school. There was no way any of them could concentrate on mid-terms today. The teachers and staff had decided to postpone exams to give the students some time to deal with the recent events. Thanksgiving was only a week away and no one wanted to worry about exams during the holiday either. In the cafeteria, Kristin and Amy were sitting together worrying. "Where could she be?" Amy said.

"All the girls were connected to us in some way, "Sam said. "We all dated them. Maybe it is someone we know. I mean maybe someone was jealous of us and is trying to get back at us for something?"

"Let's think, Kim was found near Mike's house, Calley out behind the football field, and Amanda went missing from a party after a game. It's got to have something to do with that," Kristin said.

"With what?" Mike said.

"The team you idiot! You guys are going all the way this year. How many other people are jealous as hell of you? Think about it. Ethan, you are the MVP and how easy would it be to mess up your game if they took out your good luck charm?" Amy said, grabbing Mike by the arm.

"It makes sense, but we still don't know where to look for her. She could be anywhere," Ethan said, running his hands through his hair.

"Let's make a list of anyone that might have a grudge against you guys and go from there," Amy suggested.

They all thought for a minute and came up with a few names, but one stood out to them all, John Waters. John used to be on the team until Ethan made quarterback and he was benched a few years ago. John didn't bother to try out again knowing that Ethan would take the lead. He stopped hanging around with everyone because his jealousy sent him into a rage. They all used to be friends with John when they were dating those girls. Then Kim dumped Ethan for him, Calley dated him later on and so did Amanda. John had also been interested in Sara.

"It has to be him," Kristin said.

"Let's get him before he hurts Sara," Ethan said, angry at the thought of him hurting Sara.

They all piled into their cars and headed out to John's house. Not really sure where to look for him they figured that was a good place to start. John lived on the outskirts of town on a heavily wooded lot. There was a barn out back. John's car was the only one in the driveway so they assumed he must be there. The house was silent as if no one were home. They all ran quietly toward the barn hoping to find Sara inside. Mike pushed the barn doors open and light poured in, revealing old farm equipment that hadn't been touched in years. They heard a noise toward the back of the barn. Amy and Kristin stayed back near the entrance at the barn doors while the guys went to check out the noise. As they crept toward the back of the barn they saw Amanda, bound and gagged on the dirt floor. She was struggling with the ties to free herself. Mike threw his jacket around her and they cut the ties. They helped her to her feet but she was too weak to move. Mike picked her up and they got out as quickly as possible.

"Are you hurt?" Amy asked Amanda.

"He tried to kill me. He went crazy or something. Ethan—he has Sara. He is sick. He is going to kill her too." Amanda said.

Ethan, enraged, said, "I am going after him now. You guys stay here and call Chief Grady."

"Dude, you can't go off on your own and look for him. You have no idea where he might be and what he is capable of. Let's just wait for help," Mike said.

Kristin called 911 from her cell phone and they all stayed put until Chief Grady arrived.

"You kids could have been hurt out here. What made you think of coming out here to this place?"

"Chief, we know who has Sara. John Waters lives here. We think he has a grudge against us, all of us, and he is going to hurt Sara if we don't find her," Ethan said.

"We have contacted the Waters and they don't know where John is. His parents said that he camps out in the woods often so there is no telling where he might be. We will send search teams out soon," Sara's father said, pulling Ethan aside. "I know you care for my daughter. Don't worry, we will find her."

Within an hour a search party was formed and off into the woods. Ethan, Mike, and Sam decided to do their own search hoping to cover more ground faster. It had begun to snow and the temperature was dropping fast. It was dark before they knew it and the search was called off until morning. Chief Grady gave instructions to the search parties and told everyone to be back at first light, they would resume searching then.

Back at Mike's house everyone congregated by the fire in the living room. Amy was sitting on the floor in front of Mike with her arms wrapped around her knees. Kristin was snuggled next to Sam on the couch. Ethan was pacing the room.

"Do you remember when we all went camping one summer on the ridge?" Mike asked.

"Yeah, do you think John took her there?" Sam said.

"It's worth a shot. We will leave at first light," Mike said.

No one could sleep that night. Ethan was a wreck just waiting for daybreak. Amy and Kristin had gone home while the guys stayed behind at Mike's.

The next morning the snow had stopped but the temperature had fallen to below freezing and everything was covered in a crusting of ice. The guys headed up a long winding hill deep into the woods outside of Simpleton. The ridge was a sheer rock formation that overlooked the valley that Simpleton was nestled in. The ground was slick from the snow. The air was cold and hurt their lungs from running. As they got closer to the top of the ridge they heard muffled screams. It was Sara for sure. They picked up the pace trying to secure their foothold and not fall off the edge of the ridge. When they approached the top they saw them, John and Sara. Sara was bound and gagged; she had dried blood on her face from a head wound. She was crying and struggling to free the ropes from her hands. John's back was to them as they silently made their way toward the top. After they all safely positioned themselves on the ledge, Ethan yelled, "John, what are you doing?"

John spun around fast. He had a crazed look in his eyes; eyes black like he was possessed. "Stay where you are. You can't save her, Ethan. She is going to die like the rest of them. You did this; if you hadn't come along I would be MVP."

"Look—let's talk this through, no one else has to get hurt," Ethan said. Mike and Sam were inching their way toward her. Sara had fear in her eyes and Ethan saw it.

"You don't know what it has been like. One minute everyone looks up to you and then you come along and took my place, so I figured I would take your girls. Sara here is just the icing on the cake. If I can't have her, no one will," John said, pushing her toward the edge of the ridge. Sara's feet were bound so she fell hard against the rocky edge. The ropes had cut into her hands and she was bleeding badly again. Ethan's temper was rising. Someone had to do something fast or she would fall off that ridge.

"John, you are right man. It's all my fault that this happened," Ethan tried to placate him. "Blame me, not Sara."

"You are right, it is your fault," John said as he lunged for Ethan. They knocked each other to the ground. Sam and Mike tackled John and held him down. Ethan got one good punch in to his jaw and knocked him out cold. Ethan ran to Sara trying his best to untie the ropes. There was so much blood and Ethan knew if Sara didn't get those cuts covered Sara was going to be in serious condition and possibly bleed out completely.

"We have to hurry, Sara needs help," Ethan said. Mike and Sam dragged John while Ethan lifted Sara's semiconscious body off the ground. They started back down the hill and that is when they heard the search party. They began yelling to get the searchers' attention and help came fast.

Chief Grady asked, "How did you find her?"

"We spent a summer up here camping when we were kids. We figured this is where he might take her," Mike said.

Paramedics came and took Sara from Ethan's arms. She needed stitches to close the wounds so they were taking her to the hospital. Sara also had a mild case of hypothermia from being in the cold all night.

"He admitted to killing those girls and hurting Amanda. He was going to kill Sara too. John wanted revenge and just snapped," Ethan said, trying to figure everything out.

Sara's dad put his hand on Ethan's shoulder and said, "That's not important now. You found my daughter and she is safe. Thank you."

Chief Grady handcuffed John and everyone headed back toward the clearing. "I am going to need statements from all of you about what happened."

"Can we go to the hospital first?" Ethan asked.

"Sure thing, but afterward please come by the station."

Chapter 14

Sara woke up in the hospital with bandages around her wrists and forehead. She had lost a lot of blood so they gave her a transfusion. Sara needed several stitches to close the gash in her forehead from where she had fallen on the rocks. The doctors said she would be fine but might have a small scar and that the transfusion would help the anemia problem.

There was a soft knock on the door, "Hey girly, how are you doing?" Amy said stepping inside the room. Kristin, Sam, and Mike followed her in.

"A little banged up but I will be good as new soon."

"We were so worried about you," Kristin said.

"We found Amanda, she is alive," Amy said.

"You guys were amazing. You saved my life. I don't know how to thank you."

"Foot rubs and massages sound pretty good to me," Mike joked and Amy elbowed him in the ribs.

"What is going to happen to John?" Sara asked.

"He confessed to murdering those girls and kidnapping and attempted murder of Amanda. He just snapped," Mike said.

"He set up Mr. Stone. He didn't have anything to do with it. Your dad released him earlier today," Sam said.

"I wonder what is going to happen to him. Do you think he will come back to Simpleton?" Kristin asked.

"Where is Ethan?" Sara said, worried that something had happened to him.

"He will be here soon. Your dad made everyone give statements," Amy said.

"That figures, always doing his job," Sara said.

"We will let you rest. I will come by tomorrow to check on you," Amy said hugging her. They all left together. Sara was so lucky to have met them. They were her best friends.

A short time later, Ethan arrived with a bouquet of red roses. Sara's face lit up when she saw him.

"Hey sweetness."

"Ethan, I can't thank you enough for what you did," Sara said sitting up in the bed.

"Shh." he said, touching his finger to her lips. Ethan sat on the bed next to Sara and brushed her cheek with his hand. "I am glad you are going to be okay. I was so worried about you. I don't know what I would have done if anything happened to you. The thought of losing you just…." He looked into Sara's eyes with a wrinkle in his brow. He kissed her lips softly and took her hands into his.

"The doctors said I can go home tomorrow."

"Well, I am not leaving you tonight. I will take you home tomorrow."

"Are my parents okay?"

"They are fine. Your mom is picking your brother up at the airport; he flew home when he heard you were hurt. Your dad has been working nonstop."

"Brian is coming?" Sara said happily. "You know, he is protective of me. He might want to beat you up or something," Sara said, laughing. It hurt her side, still really tender from the bruises.

"What for?" Ethan said.

"For letting his little sister fall in love with you." Sara reached for his hand. Ethan leaned in and kissed her again.

Sara put her hand to her neck and noticed the chain was gone. "Ethan, your ring. It must have fallen off somewhere. I am so sorry," Sara said feeling horrible that it was lost.

"Sara, I don't care about that ring. You are more special to me than anything." Ethan stayed with her that night and the next day until she was released from the hospital.

When they arrived at Sara's house the next day, Brian gave Sara a big bear hug and said, "I told you to be careful now didn't I?"

"Shut up you dork," Sara said punching him in the arm.

"Mom has been cooking up a storm since yesterday. She thinks I have gotten too thin and wants to fatten me up."

"Um, Brian, I want you to meet Ethan," Sara said shyly.

"Thanks for saving my baby sister," Brian said to Ethan.

They shook hands and went inside together.

John was committed to the state mental hospital for treatment because he was found mentally unfit to stand trial for the mountain of charges against him. Apparently, he recanted his confession after being arrested. No one really spoke much about what happened much after that. Sara was not sure if her life would ever be normal in Simpleton after all that had happened.

Chapter 15

December came with the coldest temperatures in history. Simpleton High won the state championships and Ethan was voted MVP. He was being recruited by a bunch of big name schools to start as quarterback as a freshman.

Snow had covered the ground. It was Christmas night. Ethan and Sara had spent the day with family celebrating the holiday. Brian brought Samantha home to meet the family. Sara and Samantha hit it off great and their mom was in love with her too. Apparently they were pretty serious and were talking about moving in together next year. Needless to say their parents weren't thrilled about it, but Samantha seemed like such a nice person they didn't worry too much. Sara was so happy for Brian, he'd finally found someone.

The 'group'—as Sara often referred to her best friends—had been planning a long weekend skiing trip up to Mike's parent's chalet in the mountains for weeks now. Sara's parents were not crazy about the idea of her going away unsupervised for a weekend, but they trusted her and it was Christmas. Sara was home packing some warm—and some not so warm—things. Ethan and Sara decided to wait until they were alone to exchange presents. She had wanted to do something special for Ethan since all they had been through together. She had bought him a Tag Heuer watch, one that he had seen a while back and loved. It cost a small fortune, but he was worth it. She had inscribed on the back, *That Night* and the date of Homecoming.

Ethan borrowed his parents' Chevy Tahoe with four-wheel drive to be sure they all made it safely to the mountains. The drive was long and it snowed most of the way. With the exception of Mike, they all rode together to the chalet. Mike had gone up early to celebrate Christmas with his family and was waiting for them to arrive. The house was incredible—like something out of a magazine. The group pulled into the circular drive and piled out. The guys took the skis down and got them ready for a night run. Amy, Kristin, and Sara went into the house and out of the cold.

"This place is enormous!" Amy said. The house was decorated to the hilt. There was a 15 foot tree in the den totally decked out for the holidays. There were holly branches and evergreen spiraling the banisters and staircases. A stone fireplace was roaring between the kitchen and den, warming the house. The house was not unlike Mike's lake house with one side entirely made up of windows. The snow blanketed the mountains and everything was peaceful.

After an enormous feast of baked ham, mashed potatoes with mozzarella, sweet baby carrots and the most delicious yeast rolls, they sat down to exchange presents. Sara gave Amy and Kristin cashmere sweaters with matching scarves. They gave her a photo book of the senior year and the cheerleading squad adventures. Mike gave Ethan and Sam a Nintendo Wii. As if the house and the weekend weren't enough, Mike gave the girls gift certificates to the spa down the road for a day of manicures, pedicures, and massages. Amy and Mike were really going strong. Like Ethan and Sara, they were inseparable. Mike and Amy had both been accepted to Notre Dame next year and Sara was a little jealous of them. Sam was off to Penn State and Kristin to Stanford. Sara was still waiting on her acceptance to Harvard and Ethan was trying to decide which school would offer him the best scholarship. His parents had been pressuring him to make a decision soon and it was still a sore subject between them.

After all the exchanging was done—except Ethan and Sara had yet to exchange gifts—Mike dropped the bomb. "Amy, there is one more present I wanted to give you this Christmas."

Ethan and Sam were in on it. They turned the lights down and let the candles and fireplace sparkle in the dim light of the evening. Mike got down on his knee in front of Amy and pulled a little black box out and held it in his hand. Kristin and Sara looked in shock at each other.

"You know I love you and can't imagine what my life would be like without you," Mike said. Amy was holding her breath and looked past Mike at Kristin and Sara. Sara mouthed the word *breathe* to Amy, as Amy had done for her so long ago now. "Will you marry me?" Mike asked her, opening the box to reveal a diamond ring.

"Oh My....Yes, Yes, Yes!" Amy said and grabbed Mike around the neck. He kissed her and slid the ring on her finger. Kristin and Sara just about tackled them because they were so happy and shocked by this turn of events. Ethan and Sam congratulated Mike and Amy and they all decided to go for a night run.

The skiing was fantastic. The snow was perfect and although it was cold, the moonlit sky and everything seemed untouched and perfect like a dream. By the time everyone made their way back to the chalet it was around midnight they were all exhausted. Sara was frozen through many layers of clothes. Mike gave the grand tour and showed everyone to their rooms. Ethan and Sara hadn't been alone in so long Sara felt a sudden nervousness in her stomach. The room they were going to stay in had an enormous four post king sized bed that needed a step stool to get up into. The bathroom had a Jacuzzi tub for two and a shower that had water jets coming out of the walls and a waterfall shower head. Their bags had been brought to the room. Sara went into the bathroom and started the shower.

"I am going to shower and warm up," she said to Ethan.

"OK, do you want some company in there?" Ethan said, smiling.

"I think I will be fine for now, maybe later," Sara said, closing the door behind her.

Amy and Sara had gone shopping a few weeks ago for their Christmas presents and she had helped Sara pick out something especially for that night. It was a white silk teddy. Amy pushed for a garter, but Sara knew it wasn't her style. After standing in that amazing shower until her skin was pink and hot, she dried off, pulled her hair into a knot and secured it with a stick. She put on some lavender scented lotion and dabbed her favorite perfume behind her ear, between her breasts, and at the back of each knee. She looked at herself in the mirror and said to herself, *Hope he likes his present.* Sara turned off the lights and slid open the bedroom door. Ethan had started a fire and lit candles in the room. He was lying on the bed with his shirt unbuttoned. He looked toward the doorway at her as she crossed the room toward where he was laying.

"Merry Christmas Ethan." Sara stood shyly in the firelight. They hadn't been together since Homecoming night. They just felt it was best to wait again despite being in love. He lifted her onto the bed and on to his lap. He put his arms around her and held her close smelling her neck and running his nose gently up to her ear.

"Now this is what I call a Christmas present," he whispered into Sara's ear.

"Oh this old thing," she said with a laugh.

"Can I unwrap you now, or do I have to wait?" Ethan asked, kissing her neck. Sara pushed his shirt off his shoulders and pulled him close. His skin tasted salty and his hair was damp from the snow outside.

"I am so happy for Amy and Mike," Sara said, trying to distract him and prolong the moment. Truthfully, she was a bit nervous. It had been so long since they had been this close and alone without distractions. Trying not to ruin the mood Sara asked him, "Would you like your present now?"

"Um…is this a trick question?" Ethan said running his hands down her back. Sara handed him the box wrapped up with a red bow and his eyes lit up. Ethan opened the box and said, "Sara, you shouldn't have." He took the watch out of the box and put it on his wrist.

"I am glad you like it, I wanted you to have something to always remember me by when you are away at school next year," Sara said, trying not to sound disappointed by Amy and Mike's incredible news.

"You already gave me that, remember?" he said pulling her close and softly kissing her.

"How could I ever forget that night? It was the best night of my life," Sara said, thinking back to the way he made her feel. Shivers ran down her spine and goose bumps appeared on her skin.

"Are you cold, sweetness, because I can think of a way to warm you up," Ethan said with a smile. Sara kissed him softly on the lips. His lips were soft and warm and his breath was hot when he opened his mouth and gently touched his tongue to hers. Sara let her hands roam his beautiful body. She tilted her head back and sighed with pleasure. Suddenly, Ethan stopped kissing her and said, "So do you want your present now?"

"That depends on what it is," she said seductively. He put his hand under his pillow and pulled out two envelopes and handed them to her.

"What is this?"

"Open them."

Sara turned the envelopes over and there was the Harvard seal on top of each one. They were acceptance letters, one with Sara's name and the other with Ethan's name printed on top. Ethan had applied to Harvard and was accepted with a full athletic scholarship. Her eyes lit up and she tackled him onto his bed. Sara was so happy at that moment. Not only did she get accepted, which was the best news of her life, but they would be together next fall.

"Wow, I wasn't expecting that reaction," he said with surprise kissing her nose.

"I just am so happy. I didn't know what would happen next year and now I know everything will be fine."

Sara lay back on the bed staring up at him. "I have one more present for you," he said softly.

"What could you possibly give me that could top this present?" Sara said, lifting the acceptance letter. She had waited her entire life to hold that letter in her hands. It was like all her dreams had come true in that moment.

"Just this," Ethan said, pulling a little black box out from under his pillow.

Sara looked at him and at the box. Her stomach was filled with butterflies.

"Open it." He grinned from ear to ear.

Sara lifted the lid and saw the most beautiful ring. It was silver with a sapphire in the center surrounded by small round diamonds. It sparkled in the candlelight. Sara was speechless once again.

"I figured this one would fit better than the last."

"It's beautiful," Sara said with a tear in her eye.

"Sara, I know we are young and have a whole life ahead of us. I promise that I will always be with you if you will have me."

"Yes, oh Ethan, I love you so much," Sara said as he placed the ring on her left hand.

"Sara, I love you more than anything. I knew you were the one for me when I saw you in the cafeteria that first day you came to school. I would do anything for you. I want us to be together forever and I will do everything to make you happy. This ring is my promise to you." Sara hugged him tightly as tears streamed down her face.

"Sweetness, why are you crying?"

"I am the luckiest person to have someone as wonderful as you. I never thought I had a chance with someone like you when we first met. I was convinced there was something wrong with me when you waited so long to kiss me, but now I know that all good things come to those who wait. I think we have waited long enough, don't you?" Sara pulled him to her and kissed him passionately. They made love in the firelight. Afterwards—their bodies glistening with perspiration—they laid in each other's arms.

"I thought my present was going to be the best part of the night," he said in her ear.

Sara smiled and rolled over to kiss him. "I love you Ethan."

"Words cannot express how much I love you Sara Grady."

“Then why don’t you show me,” Sara said with a wicked smile and rolled back on top of him. They fell asleep at some point.

Sara woke when it was still dark out and watched Ethan sleeping soundly. She went to the bathroom and drew a hot bath, lit the candles around the tub and slid into the vanilla scented world of pure bliss. She closed her eyes and replayed the events of the night and of everything that had happened since they met. How could she be so lucky? *Me ,of all people, finding true love*, she thought. Ethan came into the bathroom and slid into the water beside her.

“You left me all alone in that great big bed. I figured you might want some company in here,” Ethan said. Things got pretty hot again in the steamy water of the bath tub. Sara had never done so many erotic things in her life. Ethan was so gentle with her. They got out of the tub, wrapped themselves in the warms robes and fell asleep by the fire.

They woke up around 10:00 the next morning. The guys were planning a day of snow mobiling while Kristin, Amy, and Sara were off to the spa. After hours of pampering separately, the girls finally sat alone in the sauna and chatted.

“I have big news for you both,” Sara said. “Ethan and I got into Harvard together!” she said jumping up and down. They screamed and hugged.

“That is fantastic,” Kristin said.

“So what did Ethan give you for Christmas besides multiple orgasms?” Amy asked with a giggle.

“This,” Sara said, holding her hand out to them to see the ring on her left hand.

“Oh my gosh! Are you engaged too?” Kristin asked.

“No, it’s a promise ring though. We are going to college together and whatever else the future might bring,” Sara gushed.

Amy hugged her and said, “I am so happy for you. You guys are my best friends; I am going to miss this next year.”

They enjoyed the rest of the weekend together, spending quality girl time together. They skied, ate delicious food, and spent the best times of their lives together in that snowbound wonderland.

Chapter 16

The winter was long and cold, but somehow Sara managed to make it through. Since football season and the endless practices were finally over and college was pretty much locked in for all of the group, life was pretty slow in Simpleton. Sara had managed to keep her grade point average nearly perfect with the exception of biology and there was no getting around that B, even with Ethan's help. After the holidays they began seriously planning for college next fall. Ethan's parents were thrilled with his decision to go to Harvard and major in pre-med. Sara and Ethan's relationship was better than ever.

Then late one night in May the phone calls started again.

Sara was prepping for finals. The prom and graduation were just around the corner. Her cell phone rang and she answered, "Hello." No response on the other line but she could hear someone breathing. Panic rose in her throat. Caller ID came back to an unknown number so she hung up. A few hours later it happened again. *It couldn't be the same person that was calling, could it?* Sara turned the phone off and went to bed.

The next day on her way to school Sara turned her cell phone on and had a message which she figured was from Ethan after she had turned it off the night before. However, when she checked the voicemail it was just someone breathing heavily on the other end again. Sara was freaked out and knew she would have to say something to Amy to see if maybe the guys were up to some kind of sick joke. There was no way this was happening again.

"Did you get a heavy breathing call last night?" Sara asked Amy as they stood by the lockers outside first period english.

"What are you talking about? Someone is pranking you?" Amy asked.

"I guess. I had a few calls last night and then a two minute message of heavy breathing when I turned it on again this morning."

"I am sure it was one of the guys just being stupid. They need to grow up, we are seniors."

"Yeah, maybe you are right. I am sure it's nothing," Sara said and closed her locker. Sara went on about her day and met Ethan later in biology. Finals were coming up soon and she needed some extra lab time. Sara decided to stay after class and practice some of the old labs with a few other people that seemed to be in the same boat as she was and not confident about the final exam. Around 4:30, Sara headed to her car and saw a note tucked under the windshield wiper. Figuring it was from Ethan telling her how much he loved her, Sara pulled the note off the windshield and got into the car without looking at it first. She started the engine and rolled the windows down. The air was warm and felt good on her face. She opened the note and dropped it in her lap. It read *I am watching you* in red ink. *Was this someone's idea of a sick joke?* Sara called Ethan and put her car in drive.

"Hey sweetness, finished already?" Ethan answered.

"Did you or one of the guys leave a note on my car?" Sara asked him.

"A note? No. What does it say?" Ethan said. Sara was driving fast, headed toward his house.

"It says *I am watching you* and it's written in red ink. I don't think this is funny especially after those heavy breathing phone calls and hang-ups from last night," Sara said angrily as if he was in on it.

"Wait, someone was calling you last night and then you found a note on your car today?" Ethan repeated what she had just told him, trying to put the pieces together.

"Yes, and I don't appreciate whoever is trying to scare me either," Sara said.

"Where are you?" Ethan asked, concern in his voice.

"I am headed to your house; I am about a block away."

"Is anyone following you?"

Looking in her rearview mirror Sara suddenly got freaked out and hit the accelerator. "I don't think so but meet me in the driveway anyway."

"Don't turn off the engine; we are going to see your dad right now," Ethan said. She pulled into his driveway and he was standing there waiting for her. He got in and said, "Go to the police station now. We need to find out if John is still in that mental hospital."

Sara hadn't even thought about that possibility. She started breathing funny and feeling really anxious. They pulled into the lot and headed inside. The receptionist buzzed her dad quickly and he appeared in the doorway a moment later.

"Sara, Ethan; what's up kids?" Sara's dad asked.

"Chief Grady, have you received any word that John Waters has been released from that nut house?" Ethan asked him.

"Released? Now why would you think that?"

"Dad, someone has been calling me and hanging up, leaving messages with nothing but heavy breathing and then today there was a note on my car that said someone is watching me. It's just like before when all those girls went missing," Sara said, hysterical.

"Hold on a minute, why haven't you told me about this before now?"

"I don't know. I just thought it was a prank or something until I found that note today."

"Come into my office and let me make some calls," her dad said.

They followed him into his small office. It was sparsely furnished with an old desk and chair, a small folding table that held a coffee station, a few pictures on his desk, along with his computer, an ancient telephone and a white board on the wall. Her dad picked up the phone and contacted the administrator for the state mental health facility and started inquiring about the current status of John Waters. Ethan and Sara sat in the uncomfortable wooden chairs and tried to gather what the person on the other end of the telephone was telling her dad. After a few minutes and a few one answer responses, her dad hung up and said, "Well, they are going to check and get back to us, but I am sure there is nothing to worry about."

"Chief let's just say John didn't get out. What do you think we should do about these things that are happening to Sara? Should we just ignore them, think of them as a prank and go on about our daily routines?" Ethan asked.

"Ethan, I know you and Sara have been through a traumatic year. Frankly its one for the record books if you ask me. Let's not jump to any conclusions until we hear back from the hospital staff."

Sara just sat there quietly thinking that maybe her dad was right. Maybe Ethan was just being overly cautious. *How could John escape and go unnoticed and wouldn't we be the first to be notified if he had indeed gotten out?* Sara couldn't make that feeling in the pit of her stomach go away despite trying to think about this rationally.

"Why don't you two get out and have some fun? You are only seniors—a few more weeks and then it's off to the real world. Sara, tell you mother I will be home in time for dinner tonight," Dad said as they got up to leave his office.

They left the police station and headed over to Mike's house. Spring had bloomed and all the trees were covered in flowers. The air smelled sweet with perfume as they rode with the windows down. As they pulled into the long drive, Sara saw Amy's car parked in front of the house. Ethan parked and went down by the lake where Mike and Amy were laying out catching some rays of sunshine.

"Hey guys," Amy said happy to see them. "The weather is amazing today, isn't it?"

"What's up dude, you look pissed off," Mike said to Ethan.

"Dude, be totally honest with me. Are you and the guys playing a joke on Sara?" Ethan said with a serious tone.

"No man, why? What's up? Amy mentioned the hang-ups to me earlier but I told her it wasn't me," Mike responded standing up and giving Ethan his full attention.

Ethan told them what had happened and that her dad was checking into John's whereabouts.

"Oh my gosh, do you really think John is out?" Amy asked.

"We don't know yet," Sara said feeling her stomach flare up again.

"Come on, let's go grab some food at Jasper's and forget about this. I am sure it's nothing," Mike said, pulling Amy to her feet and heading back toward the house.

Sara called her mom on the way to Jasper's to tell her she wouldn't be home for dinner and that dad would be on time.

"Have fun and tell Ethan I said hello," Mom said.

"Have you heard from Brian today? I wonder how he did on his finals," Sara asked her.

"He will probably call you before he calls us anyway," Mom said.

"See you later," Sara said and hung up as they pulled into the parking lot of Jasper's. It was really crowded today. The four of them found an empty table near the back and sat down. Mike ordered a ton of food, but Sara wasn't hungry. She was too preoccupied with what was going on at the moment.

"So have you decided where we are going for our last hurrah before we head off to college this summer?" Amy asked Sara.

"No, do you have any ideas?"

"I was thinking we could go to Europe for a few weeks, you know back pack it," Amy said.

"I love that idea. I have always wanted to go to Italy especially," Sara said with some enthusiasm.

"Too bad Mike's parents don't have a villa over there or we could have had someplace nice to crash," Amy said.

"Have you heard from Kristin today?" Sara asked her.

"Funny that you mentioned it, but no. I got the impression earlier that things were not that great between her and Sam lately so maybe they are off somewhere together."

Kristin and Sam were going to different schools across the country from one another so it was hard for their friends to imagine how they were going to make their already rocky relationship last. After the holidays Kristin had started to see Sam for who he really was, a controlling and very jealous jock, and her feelings toward him began to change.

"Why don't I step outside and try to call her and let her know we are all here?" Sara suggested.

"Sounds good, and tell her to get her butt out here soon," Amy said sipping her iced tea.

Sara stepped outside, thankful for a moment of peace, and dialed Kristin's cell. After a few rings she picked up.

"Hello," Kristin answered sounding sad.

"It's Sara, what's wrong?" Sara asked fearing the worst: that she and Sam had broken up.

"Oh Sam and I got into a wicked fight over nothing. Someone has been calling me leaving heavy breathing messages on my phone and Sam got all mad and accused me of cheating on him. Can you believe him?" She said sounding frustrated.

"Wait, you are getting calls too?" Sara asked her. Kristin didn't know about what was going on but this was way too coincidental that she was also getting these calls.

"Come to Jasper's, we are all here hanging out and I want to talk to you about something important," Sara said.

"Is Sam there?" Kristin asked.

"No, we thought you guys might be together and wanted to invite you to come join us," Sara said.

"I'll be there soon. If Sam comes and starts anything I am out of there," Kristin said. Sara stood in the parking lot looking around for who knows what before making her way back into the crowded and noisy restaurant. A little while later Kristin came in and joined them. Sara waited to say anything else until she got there.

"Where's Sam?" Ethan asked.

"Don't know and I don't care at this point," Kristin responded.

Ethan gave Sara a questioning look. Sara just shook her head indicating she would go into more detail later.

"Guys, Kristin is getting the phone calls too. It isn't just me," Sara said.

"When did they start Kristin?" Amy asked.

"Just a few days ago and that is when Sam started acting all weird and accusing me of cheating on him. He thinks that I am dating whoever keeps calling me. He doesn't believe me when I tell him that I have no idea who it is," Kristin said.

"The calls started again around the same time with me and then I found this note today after I stayed late in biology," Sara said handing the note to Mike.

"Do you think it is someone just messing around now?" Sara asked Ethan. He sat there with a puzzled look on his face uncertain how to respond. They finished eating and Ethan decided to go home with Mike and see if they could get in touch with Sam and fill him in.

"I will call you later, but please call me if you get another call from whoever this is," Ethan said kissing Sara and then getting into Mike's car.

Sara drove home and pulled into the driveway. Mom had all the windows open airing out the house from the long, stale winter.

Sara dropped her keys on the counter and called out, "Mom, Dad, I am home."

"We are in the dining room," Mom replied.

Mom had made her favorite Indonesian chicken dish for dinner and Dad was polishing off a slice of lemon meringue pie. "That was delicious Molly," Dad said.

"I have some great news, I entered one of those cooking contests and my recipe has made it to the semi-finals," Mom said.

"Mom, that is great, I think you will win for sure," Sara said smiling and sitting down at the table.

"Just don't leave me when you are a rich and famous cook," Dad said putting the last fork full of pie into his mouth.

"Oh hush you two," Mom said blushing. Her mom shared Sara's sensitive fair complexion that was a dead giveaway to their emotions.

"Dad, did you hear anything back from that administrator?" Sara asked eagerly.

"No Sara. Don't worry, if something is wrong I will tell you," he said without saying too much. He didn't want to worry her mother after all they had gone through this past fall. Her dad's job was tough on everyone, especially when it hit home the way it had done.

"Well, I am beat. I am going to shower and study before hitting the sack," Sara said getting up from the table and heading up to her room. She put the cell phone in the charger and went to shower. Not long after she was standing in the shower and shaving her legs she heard the phone ring. Sara figured it was Ethan calling so she finished what she was doing and decided to call him later. She couldn't get her head into the studying mode and decided to watch some television before hitting the sack, completely forgetting to check her phone. Around 10:30 it rang again, interrupting a movie she was interested in.

"Hello," Sara answered absently. She was greeted by heavy breathing again.

"Who is this?" Sara demanded. Still no response from the caller on the other end. Sara checked the caller ID again, but it said unknown caller.

"I am hanging up now, stop calling me," Sara said and ended the call.

A minute or so later it rang again. Not waiting to see the number on caller ID she said, "Stop calling me!"

"Wait, Sara, it's me, Ethan."

"Oh Ethan, I am sorry. I got another phone call just a minute ago. Just more heavy breathing."

"Did you see a number on your caller ID?"

"No. Did you get in touch with Sam?"

"Yes and he was really stubborn about the whole thing. He thinks you are covering for Kristin," Ethan said.

"He is such an ass. Like I want all this stress in my life again."

"Don't worry about him. Do you want me to come over?"

"My parents are home. I don't think they would like a late night booty call even if they are in love with you."

"I am serious, Sara. How about I pick you up tomorrow? I don't want you staying late without me again. At least not until we figure out who the hell is doing this."

"Love you."

"Me too sweetness. Bye." Sara turned off the ringer and put the phone on vibrate and under a pillow so she wouldn't hear it if it rang again.

Sara was hoping they would hear something about John the next day and didn't want to keep bugging her dad about it. But as luck would have it, the rest of the week went by and still no word from the hospital administrator. Kristin hadn't gotten any more calls either so maybe whoever was doing this had started to give up trying to scare them. Sam and Kristin had patched things up for the time being, but their relationship was like a time bomb waiting to explode. The weather for the weekend was supposed to be warm and sunny. Mike invited everyone to his house for a barbecue on Saturday. All of the seniors were getting antsy and ready for finals to be over and for graduation. Ethan had been persistent about not letting her go out alone and Sara was looking forward to driving her car up to the lake for the weekend. Sara packed a few things including the dreaded swim suit. She was so in need of a tan. Amy called Sara as she was headed out the door.

"Sara, have you left yet?" Amy asked.

"I am on my way, why?"

"I just got my period and forgot tampons; would you mind terribly bringing me some?"

"No problem girly, ugh what a damper on your weekend."

Sara drove into town, a minor detour, and went into the pharmacy to get what Amy needed. She said hello to Ethan's parents and they wished her a good weekend. They were really sweet people and worked really hard. Sara knew Ethan didn't want to let his father down by not following in his footsteps after college, but she also thought he needed to follow his dreams. Sara wasn't in the store more than a few minutes and headed back toward her car when she noticed something on the window. It was a note. Sara pulled it off the wiper blade and opened the door, put her keys in the ignition and started it up while looking around to see if anyone was watching. The note read *Don't forget I am still watching you.* Sara swallowed hard and pulled out of the parking space fast, hitting the accelerator. She picked up her cell and called Mike's hoping Ethan was already there. After a few rings Mike answered out of breath.

"Yo," Mike said huffing and puffing.

"What are you all out of breath for?"

"Sara, sorry we were all outside and I forgot the phone. Want to talk to your boy?" Mike said.

"Yes," Sara said trying to sound normal.

"Hold on one second," Mike said and called out to Ethan. A few more seconds passed and Ethan got on the phone.

"Hey, where are you?" Ethan said.

"On my way. Listen, I stopped by the pharmacy to pick something up for Amy and when I got back to my car there was another note," Sara said trying to stay calm.

"What? Did you see anyone? What did it say?" Ethan asked sounding really upset.

"No, I didn't see anyone and I got out of there as quickly as possible. It said 'Don't forget I am still watching you.'"

"Just be careful and get here as soon as you can," Ethan said and hung up.

Back at Mike's house, Ethan told everyone what was going on. Sam spoke up first, "So, you guys were not lying to me. Someone is really stalking the girls?"

"Yes you jerk," Kristin said punching Sam in the arm.

"Ow, that hurt," Sam said rubbing his arm.

"Where is Sara now?" Amy asked.

"She is on her way. We are calling her dad when she gets here and I am not joking around this time. If I don't get some answers, I am going down to that hospital myself to see if John is really there," Ethan said, anger in his voice.

Sara pulled into Mike's driveway fast, leaving a cloud of dust in her wake. Ethan was waiting as she parked and cut the engine.

"Call your dad now."

Sara picked up her cell and had begun to call when a picture message came in. It was a photo taken from a cell phone of Sara reading the note on my car outside the pharmacy in town earlier. Ethan grabbed the phone and said, "This has got to stop now." He called Sara's dad himself.

"Chief Grady, its Ethan. Look, here is the situation. Sara and her friend Kristin are getting stalked by someone and it has got to stop. You have to call someone and find out if that bastard Waters is still locked up in that nut house."

"Where are you kids?" Chief Grady responded.

"We are at Mike's house for the weekend." Ethan replied.

"Good, stay put and if anything changes I will contact you."

Ethan hung up and told her what her dad said. They went to join the rest of the party. Amy and Kristin were in the kitchen helping to prepare some food when they walked in. Sara handed Amy the bag with the tampons and she thanked her. Ethan went outside to be with the guys.

"This has got to stop. What did I do to deserve this?" Sara said practically breaking down in the kitchen.

"Hey, stop crying. Everything is going to be fine. We are all together and no one is going to let anything happen to any of us. Friends stick together and watch each other's back," Amy said rubbing Sara's back.

"I know, you are right. I am just feeling a little overwhelmed right now. Lots of stressful stuff is going on with graduation and finals and real life starting in just a few months," Sara said.

"Totally understandable. I mean look at my relationship with Sam," Kristin said.

"Look, let's just go out there and enjoy ourselves and stop worrying about this, okay?" Amy said.

"Deal," Sara said looking into a mirror and wiping the mascara that had run down her cheek.

By mid-afternoon the entire team had arrived and about half the senior class. The party was in full swing. There was food everywhere you looked. People were boating on the lake and lounging on the grass. Someone had started a touch football game and in general everyone seemed to be having a good time. Amy and Sara were lying on the grass getting some sun when Sara's phone rang. Her stomach sank as she picked it up to answer. To her surprise it was Brian.

"Hey Brian, thank goodness it's just you."

"Well, that was nice of you to say. What's going on?" Brian asked. Sara filled him in on the latest and he freaked out.

"Sara, you could be in danger. What is Dad doing about this?" Brian asked.

"Everything he can, don't blame Dad. This has nothing to do with him."

"Look I am coming home in a week for the summer. You will have a permanent bodyguard attached to your hip if you are not careful, I mean it."

"How is Samantha?" Sara asked, trying to change the subject.

"Great, I think she is going to stay in Boston and find us an apartment for next fall," Brian said. Ethan saw that Sara was on the phone and came toward her.

"Brian I have to run. Talk to you next week," Sara said and hung up.

"Was that your dad?" Ethan asked.

"No, it was Brian."

"Oh, nothing yet?"

"No," Sara said and Ethan turned and went back to the game. Sara lay back down in the sun and tried to block all the horrible thoughts out of her head. She wasn't going to let whoever was trying to scare her ruin her day. The sun was getting low in the sky and evening was approaching fast. Mike lit the bonfire down by the water like that night so long ago now when Kim Randall was found in the woods. Sara heard someone up on the deck call out for a band aid and she looked up to see who it was. Bobby was standing with a towel wrapped around his hand. Sara jumped up and headed toward the house to see if she could help out. Mike didn't exactly know where the first aid kit was and was interested in finishing the football game so she went in to help find it before Bobby bled all over Mike's kitchen. Sara didn't think his parents would appreciate that kind of mess.

"What did you do?" Sara asked looking at his hand.

"I went to put something in the sink and someone had put a knife in there and I cut my hand," Bobby said. Sara thought back to earlier when Amy and Kristin were preparing the food and thought they must have left it there.

"Hold on a second and let me see if I can find the first aid kit," Sara said heading toward the bathroom.

She found the first aid kit in the bathroom medicine cabinet and brought it to the kitchen to where Bobby was standing.

"This may sting a little," Sara said trying to clean the cut with antiseptic.

"Ouch, that stuff burns."

"Oh don't be a baby, seriously." She put some antibiotic cream on it and a waterproof bandage. "There, that should hold if you don't go overboard tonight."

"Thanks."

"No problem," Sara said cleaning up the mess.

"You know, Ethan hit the jackpot when he met you," Bobby said.

"Thanks Bobby, that was really sweet of you to say."

"Do you ever think about John?" Bobby asked, his voice growing cold.

"What?"

"You heard me. I know he thinks about you," Bobby said as Sara backed out of the kitchen.

"I think I had better get back to the party. I am sure Ethan is wondering what is taking me so long in here," Sara said, turning and sprinting toward the door. Bobby was much faster than her and blocked her path.

"He told me he thinks of you often and how sweet you must taste. I mean isn't that what Ethan calls you, his sweetness?" Bobby said touching Sara's face with his bandaged hand.

"Stop it, don't touch me Bobby," Sara said shoving his hand aside.

"You see, I told you I was watching you. I am always watching you. John wanted you so badly but he got greedy. He wanted all of you and he would have gotten you if you hadn't gotten in the way," Bobby said. Sara tried to move but he pinned her to the wall. He ran his hand over her bare arm.

"Please don't touch me," Sara said shaking all over.

"I am going to do what John never got the chance to, now come on," Bobby said grabbing Sara hard by the wrist.

"Bobby, please you are hurting me."

"If you scream, I will cut you," Bobby said, pulling her toward the front of the house, a knife in the waist of his pants.

"Where are you taking me?"

"To the spot, my favorite spot. It's where we put Kim when we were through with her."

"We?" Sara stopped dead in her tracks.

"Yes, you don't think John did all that on his own now do you? I mean Kim was a fighter and she took some work before we got her to submit to us. Then we took our time with her, made her scream and when we were through with her we left her here," Bobby said.

Sara's cell phone was in her pocket and she hit the last number dialed which was Mike's house phone. Someone would answer this and hear them or at least she prayed they would. Sara was no match for Bobby. He was twice the size of her and strong. She knew if someone didn't hear this there was no way she could get away from him alone.

Mike's house phone started ringing. Amy just happened to have the cordless phone on the deck and answered. "Hello," Amy said. When she didn't get a response she almost hung up and then she heard Sara's voice. "Sara, is that you? Where are you?" Amy said. Still no response so she sat for a second and listened to what was being said.

"Oh my god." Amy said and went running toward the guys playing football.

"Guys, its Sara. Listen." She hit the speaker phone and heard Bobby's voice and what he was saying about Kim Randall.

"Holy shit, that's Bobby. What the hell?" Sam said.

"Where is Sara?" Ethan yelled as he went running toward the house. Everyone followed and began to search. Amy kept listening while the others searched.

"She is not in the house," Mike yelled from the top deck.

"Shhh, I think they are in the woods. Come back and listen," Amy said.

At this point Sara wasn't sure if she had gotten through and thought the only way to get everyone's attention was to do the one thing that Bobby said not to, scream. When Bobby finished telling all the gruesome details of how he and John hurt Kim, Sara took a deep breath and screamed as loud as she could. Bobby grabbed her by the throat and cut off her airway. Sara was gasping for air. He was so strong and was lifting her off her feet. Sara was so scared; tears were streaming down her face as she tried to breathe.

"Shut up you little bitch! I told you if you screamed I would hurt you. Don't test me," Bobby growled and tightened his grip around her throat.

Everyone had come back outside and that was when they heard her scream off in the woods. Ethan and Mike went running full speed and the others followed. It was déjà vu all over again. There was just enough sunlight left in the sky so they could see where they were going without flashlights. Sara heard them calling her name and sticks and leaves crunching underneath their feet. It seemed like forever and then she heard someone yell.

"Bobby! Let Sara go now!" Ethan yelled at him.

"Not a chance man."

"What the hell are you doing?" Mike said coming to a screeching halt. The rest of the party was close behind and Bobby knew he couldn't fight them all off. He let Sara go and she fell to the ground. She was choking and trying to get air into her lungs. Every breath felt like fire as she took enormous breaths. She coughed until she could swallow air down. Sara's throat ached from his grip.

"You don't get it man. I told you I wanted her. John wanted her too. But you had to have her all to yourself. We took Kim from you and Calley too. Hell, we were going to take them all just to prove we could and get away with it. But Sara here was too good for that. She wouldn't come quietly like I told her to. John warned her that she would get hurt but that little bitch didn't listen," Bobby said, holding the knife from the kitchen in his hand.

"Bobby, it doesn't have to be like this," Ethan said trying to get closer to him. Bobby flailed the knife in his direction. Ethan jumped back, inches from making contact with the blade.

"She is going to get what she deserves," Bobby said, pulling Sara by the arm off the ground and to her feet. He put the tip of the knife to her throat. Sara was panicked; tears were burning her cheeks. The next thing she knew she heard more voices and sounds like sirens off in the distance that she thought she must be imagining.

"Put the knife down!" Chief Grady yelled at Bobby, pointing his gun at his center mass.

Bobby turned around, wheeling Sara with him like a shield. Sara was so glad to see her father but couldn't comprehend it at that moment. Bobby pressed the blade into her skin and she felt the searing pain as the knife pierced her throat. And then it was all over in a matter of seconds after that. Chief Grady shot Bobby once in the shoulder, incapacitating his arm, and he dropped the knife. Sara fell to the ground and Ethan came running toward her. Sara was crying uncontrollably. The knife had just barely cut her and the wound was superficial. Ethan picked her up and held Sara in his arms as she cried and cried. It was finally over.

Bobby was taken into custody, arrested, and charged with aggravated assault and the deaths of Kim Randall and Calley Bishop. His confession and the number of witnesses that heard him tell what happened was enough evidence to put him away for the rest of his life. Sara clung to Ethan as if her life depended on it.

After all the excitement died down and the police left, the party had thinned considerably. Ethan assured Chief Grady he would take care of Sara. Ethan brought Sara his sweatshirt to keep warm. The night was chilly but it was warm next to the fire and with Ethan close by, Sara finally felt safe.

"I guess people just don't seem to get it. I mean you are all mine now and forever and they just need to get over it," Ethan said to Sara, trying to make her smile. He kissed her forehead.

"I guess I owe you one for saving my life again," Sara said touching her throat.

"Well, we have the rest of our lives for you to pay me back," Ethan said.

"Hey, I could use a back rub," Mike said. Everyone laughed, Amy punched him in the arm, and Sara just inched closer to Ethan where she knew that she would always be safe.

www.ingramcontent.com/pod-product-compliance
Ingram Content Group UK Ltd.
Pitfield, Milton Keynes, MK11 3LW, UK
UKHW041942190726
13854UKWH00004B/1738

9 781456 761288